by Allen Tower and Michael McLaughlin

MACK
JACK
JASON BRUBAKER
15

Satan made himself multifariously objectionable and was finally expelled from Heaven. Halfway in his descent he paused, bent his head in thought a moment and at last went back. "There is one favor that I should like to ask."

"Name it."

"Man, I understand, is about to be created. He will need laws."

"What, wretch! you his appointed adversary, charged from the dawn of eternity with hatred of his soul — you ask for the right to make his laws?"

"Pardon; what I have to ask is that he be permitted to make them himself."

It was so ordered.

— Ambrose Bierce, *The Devil's Dictionary*

Credits

Written by: Allan Tower and Michael McLaughlin
Development by: Jennifer Hartshorn and Richard E. Dansky
Editing by: Ronni Radner
Art Direction by: Aileen E. Miles and Lawrence Snelly
Art by: Jason Brubaker, Daryll Elliott and Alex Sheikman.
Cover Art: Timothy Bradstreet and Grant Goleash
Cover Design: Aileen E. Miles
Layout and typesetting by: Kathleen Ryan

Special Thanks to:

Carole "Repent, Harlanquin" Simmons, because nobody escapes the Special Thanks list.

Brad "Alpha Mail" Butkovich, for finally asking the Net all about **Wraith**.

Matt "At Least *You* Didn't Scare Me" Millberger, for putting in Developer hours on **Dark Ages**.

Ronni "Ropin' the Dreidls" Radner, for making Hanukah a little bit country, a little bit klezmer.

Michael "Sugar Mouse" Rollins, for having the sense not to play Peter Hammill in public.

Kathy "Howdy, Neighbor" Ryan, for moving over to the safe side of the parking lot.

780 Park North Blvd.
Suite 100
Clarkston, GA 30021
USA

Table of Contents

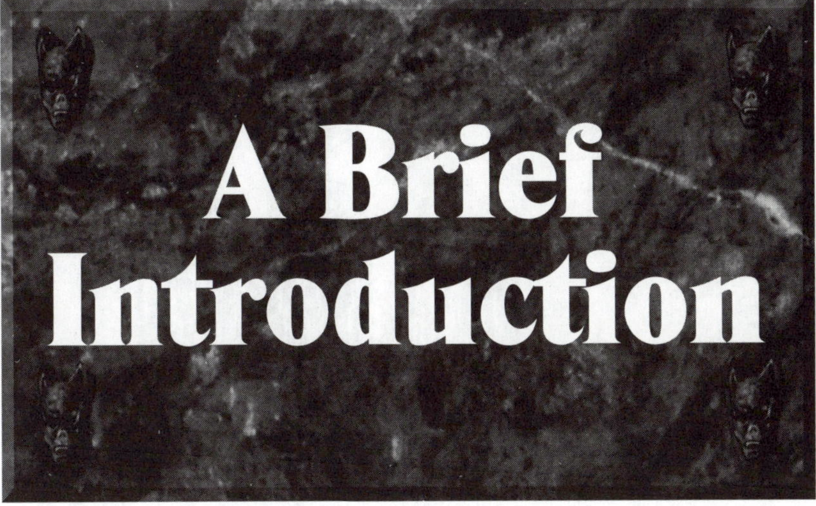

Look on my works, ye mighty, and despair.
— Percy Bysshe Shelley, "Ozymandias"

How To Use This Book

A collection of treatises, ruminations, recollections and letters on the duties and responsibilities of a prince among the Kindred, **The Prince's Primer** is intended to enlighten, inform, educate and perhaps even amuse. It is not intended as a blueprint for becoming prince, nor is it the be-all and end-all of Kindred political thought on princedom. Rather, it is a collection of opinions from both princes and their enemies on what makes a prince, and what keeps a prince in power. Its advice should be taken piecemeal, not for the gospel, and certain of our authors may have conflicting opinions on the same matter. This is just as well; what works in Washington may not play in Peoria. You may not find it useful the next time you find yourself prince of a city, with 60 ravenous Brujah in the hallway wanting to take a meeting with you. Then again, if you follow its lessons, hopefully you will never find yourself in that situation.

In any case, enjoy.

These rough photocopied pamphets have been found on several young Kindred in recent months. Word of their appearance in other cities has begun to spread as well. This particular pamphlet was found in the personal effects of a stormy young Toreador orator who had the misfortune of falling off of a 30-story building, landing in such a way that her head was removed by the impact.

K.M.G.

F. LYON WALL'S GUIDE TO

HOW THE CLANS SCREW THEIR OWN:

HOW TO BE THE LIFE OF THE PARTY

WITHOUT FOOTING THE BILL

   F. Lyon here, the Baedecker of political pitfalls for dis-
criminating bloodsuckers. Today's lesson, kids...Pay attention! I
don't want to have to rap any knuckles, not that I wouldn't enjoy
it. If I know the dark, deviant little dreams of many of you, you
wouldn't mind either, but I digress. Today's lesson is all about
getting the most from your clan while giving the least in return,
kind of like princes do. If you do it right, every day will be like a
birthday party, and all of your family will have to bring presents.
Do it wrong, though, and you become the little orphan boy who
gets treated like a servant, though some of you sick leeches might
like the idea of living a Charles Dickens story...Anyway, I'll go
through this clan by clan, bottom to top. Don't fall asleep through
the parts that you don't think concern you, because there will be a
test. It's called the rest of your unlife, and it's pass or fail.

BRUJAH

These guys live by the rule: *No one can pick on my little brother but me.* This is all well and good if there is someone from outside the family giving you grief, but that usually only happens once. Coaches always say that the body remembers what the brain forgets, and the Brujah are really good at teaching the body. School of Hard Knocks, you know. What the Brujah offer one another is a mob of well-armed thugs with bad attitude. They'll pound one another as soon as you look at them, but they close ranks tightly against outsiders. This is an invaluable asset, especially if you are dealing with members of other clans. Knowing how the Brujah treat their own, it's probably also a smart career move.

The bad thing about this mob is, well, that it's a mob. If you get anything, like maybe a position or money, the mob will want its share. There's nothing quite like a family protection racket. Brujah princes have it really rough; the mob expects free reign to go nuts and shoot up anything in sight, and to get away with it since one of theirs in on the big chair. The prince has to keep the peace, without alienating his own clan. The best way of doing that is to give them something to play with, like a nest of big hairy wolf boys. Hours of fun, and it keeps the thug pack in top fighting form. If they win, the prince gets the credit for putting down the dogs. If they lose, the prince gets credit for *trying* to put down the dogs, and everybody breathes a sigh of relief that the thugs aren't around anymore. It's not pretty, but what do you expect? We're vampires, and that word is pretty synonymous with the term "total bastard."

GANGREL

There are loners, and then there are loners. After that, there are the Gangrel. Pound for pound, there's probably no clan tougher in the entire Camarilla. Are you listening, Brujah kids? And they're sneaky, too, coming and going as they please. Real friendly, especially when two of them meet. They immediately act like old friends, but I guess nearly all of them are. They don't see much of one another, but they all seem to get along real well. Problem is, there aren't ever really very many of them in any particular place. That's the drawback to being a Gangrel; from day one you're pretty much on your own. Probably why the ones that make it are so tough.

That's also what's good about being a Gangrel. They almost never have an elder about telling them what to do, and when they do, it's usually good sense to listen. There's no one to fall back on, but there's no one to hold you back, either. It's a rare event that will draw more than a couple of these folks together, but when it happens, watch out. They've usually got their tails in a knot over something, and they're really intent on unknotting it. It may not be important to you, but it's damn important to them, and blood usually flows pretty freely. That's probably why you almost never see a Gangrel prince; most of them have wandering fever and can't stay in one place for too long. Know what they call a prince who leaves his city? An ex-prince. If you do run across one, she'll be the toughest leech for miles around, guaranteed. And she won't be happy to see a mission-driven pack of other Gangrel, either, because she'll be expected to join in the just crusade against whatever evil. Crusades are bad for princes; they damn near busted Europe, and that wasn't even in their backyards.

MALKAVIAN

Yeah, okay, it's true that Malkavians are all slightly bent, but how sure are you that you're totally sane, buster? If you're honest and not a complete idiot, that gave you pause. If not, well, time has a way of taking care of liars and fools. They usually end up being princes...But I'm not to that point yet. I'm going to tell you why sometimes it's good to be crazy, and why hanging out with cuckoos can get you down. See, if people think you're bonkers, you can get away with tons. Like this little pamphlet; who d' you think really reads this stuff? Not the elders, but the kiddies might get something good and useful out of it. Or they might get a chuckle, or something to wrap fish in. No one takes a kook seriously, so a serious kook can get a lot done so long as he acts nutty from time to time. It's a form of invisibility: out of mind, out of sight.

The bad part is the other nuts. If you get more than a few together, it turns into chaos. Everyone starts screaming for attention, and nothing at all can get accomplished. The only real thing we have in common is being a few cards short or over of 78; nothing else binds us together. If you're lucky enough to share neuroses with someone (which is much more sanitary than sharing blood), you might actually manage to get something useful accomplished. But basically, being a childe of Malkav is great around other leeches, but more than a little depressing when you're hanging out with the family. And the prince of fools? That is a rare bird indeed, and I don't mean a cuckoo. It's a thin line to walk between a working mask of insanity and having enough lucidity to function. It's been done before, and humans have certainly been known to have insane monarchs, but the stigma of being a known neurotic is hard to shake.

NOSFERATU

Yeah, so they're ugly. At least they're only ugly on the outside, which is a hell of a lot more than I can say for lots of bloodsuckers. Having to face the world as you really are does something to your perspective, I think. All the Nossies I've met have been straight up. They stick by one another, too, which is more than I can say for a lot of leeches. They're a tight-knit bunch, but it's kinda understandable; wouldn't you turn to the only people who wouldn't give you a hard time about your looks? Superficial they aren't; they can't afford to be.

Everybody knows that no one is better informed than the Nosferatu. What most folks don't know is that they all share the majority of their information with one another; it's a group protection kind of thing. So that's what the Nos do for one another; they stand up for each other, and watch out for their kind with the tools at hand. The downside of it all is their reputation, not their looks. They're like Switzerland with attitude; they don't often take sides, but when they do, head for another city. People are reluctant to trust the sewer dwellers other than for the accuracy of their information. Years of being in the trade have made them valued, but suspect outside of it. It's a tough rep to shake, but it's served a few Nosferatu princes I know of pretty well. Think about it: Would you want to go toe-to-toe with the one person who knows more about you than maybe yourself? Damn right you wouldn't. Unfortunately, they are a lonely lot, based on both their appearance and their creepy reputation. I like 'em a lot, but I couldn't imagine living like that.

TOREADOR

You know the old saying: *Keep your friends close, but your enemies closer*? If I didn't know better, I'd swear that the guy who thought it up was talking about the Tories. Sure, they're one of the respected, good-looking and well-dressed clans, but it's one hell of a price to pay. If you aren't an artist, you're already a step back. Even if you are an artist, and a damned good one, you still aren't assured of anything with this bunch. On a good day, the Tories are elegant and gracious, making the Ventrue and Tremere look like they shop out of catalogs and get their manners from reading old books. And they know how to throw a party too, if you can manage to get invited or crash without too much trouble. On a bad day, though, given my choice, I think I might rather take a beating at the hands of the Brujah (sit down, thug boy, that was only a figure of speech) than suffer through one of their very public attacks on my character. Brutal is not even a strong enough word.

So let's say you're a Torie princess — hard to think of them as anything else; even the guys are absolutely spoiled rotten — what would that mean? Well, for one thing, you'd better look, dress and act the part, or the dishers will do their worst on you. On the other hand, you would get respect if you could pull it off. Throw in extravagant art shows and you're set, at least with your own. The upside is that you get respect, or at least some degree of acceptance, if you can walk the walk. The downside is that lots of folks will assume you're either a feckless artist or a good-for-nothing gossip. In either case, they won't take you too seriously, unless you prove to them over and over that you deserve it. Being a Torie gets you in the door, but more as the entertainment than as a guest.

TREMERE

Is it cold in here all of the sudden, or is it just me? These guys (and girls: I don't mean to slight the dominatrixes of magic) have a chilly reputation for a reason. If you knew what I knew about them, you'd have trouble sleeping days. Still, somebody has to be the guide through dangerous terrain, and they don't call me F. Lyon Wall for nothing. To the new wizards on the block, the rest of the clan is your stern father figure and your worst enemy combined. If you're Tremere, you know exactly what I mean. If not, try to imagine it, and then multiply several times. In their defense, though, the Tremere do offer total, inescapable security. The only catch is that you have to play the game by the bosses' rules, and they only tell them to you after you break them. It's a rough life, but if you survive the first few decades, you come out hard, spooky and powerful. Many of you wouldn't mind the results, but I really doubt you would want to pay the price.

What the clan asks — demands, really, I was just being polite — is obedience and to put aside all of your personal goals to further the glory of the clan. If it sounds like a cult, that's no accident; the organization is a pyramid, after all. If you win anything big, you don't win jack: the clan gets it all. Screw up, though, and you find yourself standing all alone in the spotlight. I've heard of wizard princes in Europe, and I'm very glad that there's a whole ocean between me and them. Think for a second about the first one who realized that you get an entire clan (at least seven, according to my sources) as prince. If you're a rank and file member, this is great, but if you're the prince it bites hard. If any Tremere messes up, you take the heat. If you mess up, you take the heat. If something goes right, the clan gets the credit. And nobody is going to be sympathetic to the poor little prince; everyone knows older Tremere have their emotions cauterized when they sell their souls to their masters....

VENTRUE

There's blue blood, and then there's indigo. Beyond that you'll find the color of Ventrue blood. Smug doesn't even begin to describe them. Of course, if I could make people love me and dance the Charleston naked in the rain, I might be smug too. I'll have to remember that dance trick for a future occasion, but I'm just as clueless about love as your average human. I think visiting Golconda might be a more realistic occurrence, and I can sell you a map, cheap. The Ventrue clan is like a corporate package deal that you don't have a chance to reject: you get a business suit, Italian shoes, a nice car, your bank account gets surgically augmented, and you get a job with guaranteed growth potential. Unfortunately, the Ventrue usually define growth potential at a pace that a snail would find lackadaisical. They call it taking the long view and biding your time, but I've also heard it called paralyzing caution.

Money and status matter a lot to the Ventrue. They always offer one another aid if it's needed, but they have long memories, too. By the time most princes get to the big chair (yes, Virginia, most princes are Ventrue) they usually owe members of their own clan a list of favors as long as their Rolodex. It makes sense, really; why would the clan let someone sit on the throne if everyone who mattered didn't have something to gain by it? Really, though, it isn't that bad for the prince. If everyone has something to gain by your retention of your position, then they'll work to make sure you keep it. It just becomes a race to see how long you can put off repaying those favors while you're racking up a list of debts owed to you. Like a day at the races, but without Groucho and Harpo. The stakes are an awful lot higher, too. A prince who's a bad gambler could lose a lot more than his hand-tailored shirt.

Well, kids, I hope you paid attention, because you could have learned an awful lot here if you weren't careful. Like that Bacon man said, one grows wise through reading, even if it is by yours truly. There are a couple of other pithy little quotes about knowledge that I've always wanted to use, so consider this a medley of learning; knowledge is power, knowledge implies action, and knowing is half the battle.

Kids, don't read this last part; it's only for your elders and princes. F. Lyon Wall tries to please all crowds, after all.

Ellway, ellway, ellway...Ookslay ikelay ownay everyay oneway owsknay ouryay ittlelay ecretsay. Allay eythay avehay otay owknay isay ouryay anclay anday ou'reyay ewedscray. Ebay ayay astardbay, etgay eatedtray ikelay oneway. Atay atay orfay ownay.

Yflay onay ethay allway.

JEREMY LANCASTER AND ASSOCIATES, LTD.

C O N S U L T A N T S

Kansas City
Dec. 4

Dear Mr. Smith;

As per your request, here is an analysis of current operational policy and the tools by which to implement it. There are two main sections, dealing with information and humans respectively. Each section is further broken into various spheres of influence with factors for the importance of each, the cost of obtaining them at a useful level, the cost of achieving dominance and the cost for allowing others to surpass you. If this suits your needs, I look forward to working with you in the future.

Sincerely,

Jeremy Lancaster

Leadership Cost Analysis

Information

Proper intelligence has always been vital to the operation of any large conglomerate entity, whether it is a multinational corporation or a principality. In the modern age of cable television, personal telephones and computer networks, it is even more important to secure a leading edge in information. Technology has made it possible for anyone to be well-informed if they so desire; a leader must be even more knowledge-able.

Computers

Importance: Very Important. The world is rapidly becoming a computer driven society, a trend that is no longer confined to the western world. Computers have the capability to impact every aspect of our casual lives, but they are infinitely more useful and necessary for those in leadership positions.

Cost of Utility: Nominal. Computer literacy is becoming rather common-place among the middle and upper classes, making the percentage of professionals with superior knowledge all the higher. Make no mistake; you will need professionals. A teenager with a modem and a modicum of code knowledge may be able to break into a local utility's mainframe once, but cannot do so consistently. Data organization, network maintenance, information tracking and trend prediction require more stable and reliable talent. The bottom line: several professionals, a medium-sized network and online access with a relatively secure connection. Utility level in computer technology combines synergisti-cally with utility in any other field; it is much easier to track financial dealings with access to the world markets that are accessible 24 hours a day through a computer network, for example.

Cost of Dominance: High. Technology is changing faster than most can keep up with. As we are creatures used to thinking in terms of decades, if not centuries, it can be disconcerting to master new software or hardware, only to have it become obsolete within a year. Nonetheless, this is what must be done; once the tiger's tail has been grasped, it is unwise, if even possible, to let it go. It would not be prudent to commandeer ghouls, or even embrace several skilled professionals to run this aspect of your organization if it means maintaining a comfort-able ignorance yourself. Compartmentalization has to be discarded as a business strategy, especially in this field. What you do not know can hurt you and cripple your effectiveness. Even the most respected and valued underlings can find the prospect of vast resources difficult to resist. Whether this is work on some personal project, or a wholesale co-opting of your machinery for their gain and your detriment, it will impede your productivity. A fair degree of personal knowledge is vital.

Monetary cost is also high, though the shift away from mainframes has slightly lessened this. Equipment must be upgraded, as must software. An awareness of the cutting edge, as well as compatibility, is necessary. Remember the Betamax lesson; do not make the mistake of investing in superior technology that is unusable.

Cost of Neglect: Incalculable. This is a field that cannot be overlooked, no matter what. Many contemporary Kindred are at least proficient with computer technology, and many are expert. I need not remind you that the majority of anarchs are modern. Imagine what a core of dedicated anarch hackers could do to your holdings: your bank accounts, your property files, your investments, even your police records (which could be fabricated, if they do not exist). You simply cannot rely on commercial services such as banks and brokerage houses to handle these transactions for you; you must take personal responsibility to ensure the safety and efficacy of your informational empire.

Finance

Importance: Moderate to High. Remember that the majority of your work can be done by humans, even unknowingly. Money is very important to them with their short lives and limited perspectives. It is the path to temporary luxury. Consequently, it is less appealing to aged Kindred, but not totally without utility. Many of the younger Kindred still hunger for the luxuries that were denied them in life. Indulge them with a few thousand dollars; it is a pittance to you, but may buy their distraction, if not their loyalty.

Cost of Utility: Moderate. Members of our clan are eminently qualified for rulership based mostly on our facility with wealth. The foresight and monetary savvy that no doubt attracted your sire's attention will continue to serve you well. Utility for an individual with political interests is measured in seven digits, with a steady eye toward maintenance and growth. An individual in the political spotlight must have a war chest in the lower eight digits, at the very least. Again, the emphasis on steady growth and security cannot be stressed enough. Remember the lessons of unrestrained aggression and short-sightedness in Singapore; many Kindred will be recovering from that debacle well into the next millennia.

Cost of Dominance: High. Utility is simple, yet dominance requires constant vigilance. You must not only be aware of market and currency forces, but also of those beneath you who have their eyes on upward mobility. The least threatening is someone who merely wishes to gain on her own merits. It is a simple matter of bringing them into your organization, either knowingly or as an unwitting co-investor into a project or projects you control. Similarly, you can undercut their investments and interests if they should become a threat. The greatest threat comes from those who would raise themselves higher by dragging you down. This can be from the accepted practices of insider trading, market tampering as was popular in the 1980s, data piracy, or a more direct and obvious physical terrorism, such as the World Trade

Center bombing. The simplest way to avoid suffering too drastically from any single action lies in diversity and conservatism; high return investments usually carry high risk and initial costs. Regardless, it is not enough to weather these storms. To retain your position of superiority, you must ensure that others do not profit too greatly from the storms. Often the best recourse is to utilize similar methods to those of the aspiring tycoon.

Cost of Neglect: Very High. An individual may ignore finances and instead work on the currency of prestation within the Kindred community, yet a public or political figure cannot exist on these alone. Money motivates the kine, and one cannot rule a grazing area with no knowledge or control over the herd. Shows of comfortable wealth are indelibly affixed to positions of leadership, particularly to princes. It is virtually impossible to retain the position and the respect of elders and childer alike without what would be vast resources in human terms.

Nosferatu

Importance: Very High. It is a well-known and accepted fact that none in Kindred society are better informed than these malformed spies. No matter what your security measures, mechanical and human, they will be aware of your actions and plans. Your opponents will similarly be victim to this spying. To maintain rule requires accurate and timely information, and none have a larger grasp of it than the sewer dwellers.

Cost of Utility: Moderate to Fair. The Nosferatu are often capricious when dealing with enfranchised members of the ruling class, and they may require the performance of demeaning acts as well as high prices for their information. Nonetheless, perseverance and steady payment will bring the relationship into a more standard business format. They are merchants of secrets who will sell to the highest bidder. Be wary, however, when sending underlings into the sewers. Send bonded individuals when at all possible, and make it plain to them to take care in negotiations. Much can be learned from the question, often more than from the answer, and the Nosferatu are very astute observers.

Cost of Dominance: Extremely High. To dominate the informational network of the Nosferatu would require either the bonding of the undisputed leader, and keeping this bond secret from the remaining clan members, or an alliance with them. Obviously the latter is by far the easier and safer recourse; master spies, become quite easily master assassins when wronged. The cost of alliance remains quite steep, however. The other clans, in particular the Tremere and the Toreador, have nothing but disgust for the Nosferatu, even though they utilize their services as much, if not more, than the other clans. An open alliance will be politically costly due to this fact; much public opinion can be swayed. Do not expect total complicity from your own clan, either, unless you have them in an uncharacteristic and enviable position of cooperation and control. Aristocratic prejudice runs deep, but not without reason.

Cost of Neglect: Catastrophic. Assume that no one has more knowledge concerning your activities and plans than these deformed Kindred. You will have opponents, if not actual enemies, within your domain, and the reputation of the Nosferatu is well-known. You would be in the position of having enemies more informed about your actions than you are of theirs. This may be survivable if your own position is particularly strong and your opponents' uncommonly inept.

A much more daunting situation would be if the Nosferatu themselves were antagonistic toward you and your administration. If even the pretense of neutrality is gone, you will not last long unless you can build a coalition of the other clans to cripple the Nosferatu. This is no simple feat, for no one wants to destroy a valuable resource unless the price for doing so is commensurably high. Do not alienate or antagonize the Nosferatu.

Toreador

Importance: Minimal to Moderate. Many see these Kindred as reclusive artists and idle gossips, but through the course of their gossip much information can be gleaned. The majority of it concerns the social activities of the Kindred society, a vital facet of ruling. Unlike the Nosferatu, the Toreador do not usually trade this information for personal gain, but use it to the detriment of their enemies *du jour*. Nonetheless, it is an oft overlooked and valuable source for information on your contemporaries.

Cost of Utility: Low. The Toreador gossip mongers, the harpies, are more than willing to give out information that may make others look bad as long as you feign more interest in the teller than what is being told. Flattery and favor are the medium of exchange in dealing with these individuals. Take care not to tip your hand; a suspicious harpy is a resource squandered, and possibly a liability gained. Give the appearance of playing their game; indulge in meaningless gossip, or plant an agent of your own clan in their midst. Whoever engages them should develop a casual cruelty and apparent indifference to the opinions of others. Above all else, be certain to have at least a small amount of new gossip for trading purposes.

Cost of Dominance: Moderate to High. As with the Nosferatu, it would take either a bonding of a leader of the harpies, or an alliance with them. The former is a temporary measure at best, as the harpies are as vicious with one another as they are with outsiders, if not more so. Even if a bonding of a stable leader were to take place, there is still the necessity of keeping the event a secret, which is unlikely in Kindred society. Alliances may be beneficial, but not without cost. If the rift between the *artistes* and *poseurs* is large, the former may be significantly offended at an alliance, so much so that they may openly oppose you on minor points. Even if this does not occur, the disenfranchised Kindred will see this as nothing more than reinforcing the belief that princes foster the worst of Kindred society. In particular, the Brujah and Nosferatu will take particular offense at an open alliance with the harpies.

Cost of Neglect: Minimal to Moderate. By sheer virtue of being a public figure, the prince will attract negative comment, especially by gossip mongers. Do not make the mistake of mortal politicians who base all of their decisions on the probable popularity of the moment. This is the only way to truly make the harpies happy; by consulting with them before every event. Clearly, this would be the death knell of an effective prince, and even then it would not guarantee good will. The harpies are a capricious lot. They may create an atmosphere of mild disdain in those predisposed to it, but alone they cannot truly hurt you.

Humans

The primary job of a prince is to enforce the Masquerade. None would dispute this fact. Fortunately, the First Tradition can protect a prince as well as the Kindred population at large. Many human agencies exist to react to particular situations: the police react to personal and property crimes; medical facilities react to and record injuries; local government records things such as property ownership; the media reports on anything it deems "newsworthy." All four of these human agencies would react to Kindred activities, given the opportunity, and all would potentially breach the Masquerade. As prince, it is a simple thing to forbid and enforce overt manipulation of these and others in the name of mutual protection, and most would see the logic of such an act. Similarly, you can set such forces in motion against an individual or group. Such an action would force the target or targets to respond to the agency, rather than the initiator, so that the Masquerade will remain unbroken. Many will cry foul at such action, but it is a simple matter of pointing out that had the offending party not taken questionable action, there would have been no danger to investigation by the humans.

The Media

Importance: High to Very High. Humans are connected to one another via the media; he who controls the latter often controls some aspect of the former. First and foremost, the media cannot be left to its own devices; this assures difficulty in the maintenance of the Masquerade. Damage control is the fundamental use of the media. Kudos are given to he who handles these difficulties, but the prince is the only one who will be held accountable if they are not.

Cost of Utility: Moderate. Due to federal statutes, it is difficult to consolidate media companies under one simple corporate entity, though an enterprising individual can always find a way around them. This makes the task of developing and maintaining various contacts more difficult. It is not enough to dominate one company alone, or even one aspect of the media, such as the newspapers or broadcast television. It will be of little consequence that the 11 o'clock news does not carry coverage of exsanguinated corpses if it appears on the front page of the morning edition of the newspaper. To be effective in the minimally acceptable capacity, a prince must have contacts and some degree of control over all aspects of the media, or he will be forced to turn to others in this matter. If the Masquerade is at stake, most Kindred with any sense of self-protection will assist in this matter, but they will also remember that the prince could not handle these matters alone. Similarly, the media can be used to bolster one's other contacts and enterprises, and vice versa. It is a simple matter to have a police detective leak information to a reporter when both are under your influence. If a troublesome Kindred still dabbles in business or society, unflattering articles in the appropriate sections will damage her standing significantly. Be aware, however, that unless you possess dominion in the media field, this can also be done to you.

Cost of Dominance: High to Very High. In any city large enough to sustain a sizable Kindred population, there will be at least four television stations, two newspapers and numerous radio stations. Add to that the fact that reporters are by definition prone to disobey orders and pursue stories on their own initiative, and the difficulties will be obvious. Whereas one or two highly-placed staff members can stop a story at one location once, it takes many more acting in unwitting concert to substantially alter the news that the kine receive in any significant way. Many Kindred see the value of having contacts in the media, which makes the task of domination more challenging. It makes little difference if your news director gives orders that another Kindred countermands to a reporter under his control; vampires are substantially more persuasive than humans. It becomes a task of guarding against any progress being made by an individual or group into the area once you have established it as your own. This is a difficult and consuming task, but worth consideration. In clever hands, the media is a tool that cannot be rivaled.

Cost of Neglect: Catastrophic. The protection of the Masquerade is the primary role of the prince. This is virtually impossible without some degree of influence over the media. It is possible to rely on others to take care of this duty, but so doing would undermine the foundation of an active and vital princedom. With no influence at all in the various media outlets, the best that is possible is a mere figurehead position, where you are prince in name only.

Medicine

Importance: Low to Moderate. Medical influence is often overlooked, but it can prove to be a valuable asset if properly utilized. This concept seems to escape most Kindred, who view medical contacts as little more than an opportunity to obtain safe and quick, if unpleasant, sustenance. However, hospitals are required by law to record every gunshot wound that enters their doors. This provides an opportunity to suppress an incident and keep it from a wider mortal audience, or to allow it to pass on to the police and the media. Ghouls and retainers occasionally require medical attention, and their masters are often grateful. If you control all access and egress from health care facilities, their gratitude must fall to you. Finally, all hospitals have a morgue and an incinerator, making the ultimate disposal of unwanted waste a simple matter.

Cost of Utility: Low. Most metropolitan hospitals are large, disorganized and understaffed; this is even more pronounced in public facilities. These conditions make it a simple matter to gain a measure of control over at least one member of the staff, whether through bribery (nurses and orderlies are notoriously underpaid) or other, more permanent measures. In such large and chaotic environments, even control of one or two orderlies can accomplish much, from body disposal to blood storage. In more drastic cases, agents can be used to eliminate recuperating witnesses and other problematic individuals, though this may often result in the loss of the agent unless total control of the facility is yours.

Cost of Dominance: Moderate to High. It is simpler to gain control over a single institute than to achieve citywide dominance. Only the most ambitious and farsighted individuals would even contemplate the latter. When targeting dominance in a hospital, target the emergency room staff first. Do not target the doctors, but the support staff. It is they who control the tracking of patients and records, as well as admitting and stock. Indeed, if you have secured the support staff in a given area, the doctors are secondary. The administrators are also of vital importance, as they secure the funding and give orders to all staff members. It is very possible to have total control over a hospital or critical care facility without securing every doctor. Patience is vital, however; sudden control will arouse suspicion. Once the staff is yours to command, all that occurs within the walls is your domain. Blood may be stored for emergencies, bodies may be disposed of and witnesses may die on the tables. Additionally, all mortal contacts and agents of other Kindred eventually must seek medical attention. Once they set foot within your facility, you may either cripple or inconvenience the plans and opera-tions of other Kindred, or cause them to incur debt to you.

Cost of Neglect: Minimal to Low. This is an area in which diligence is not vital. The worst that can occur is if agents or tools of yours must seek treatment. Then it becomes a matter of assuring their delivery to an uncontested facility, or negotiation with those currently controlling it. Medical influence is at best extremely useful, at worst a minor inconve-nience.

Government

Importance: High. The term government is used to describe all facets of publicly controlled and regulated service. This includes, to a degree, utility providers (which fall under the public service commission), the regulatory commissions, as well as the judicial system and the publicly elected governing bodies. As a ruler, it is important to be able to control those who control the kine. This cannot be allowed to fall totally into the hands of another Kindred, for the landscape of the city itself will be against you. Decisions will be undercut by human agency. Prime feeding grounds will be devalued, quickly becoming dangerous, or the environs of Elysium will change in ways inappropriate to the atmosphere of safety. A ruler who cannot govern the kine will have difficulty gaining respect from the Kindred, who will turn their eyes to another who is more capable. Consider the operation of the human agencies in the city equivalent to Wales in regards to competence in governing. It is a test you cannot afford to fail.

Cost of Utility: Moderate to High. The price varies, depending on the level of redundancy in your city. As with hospitals, it is the support staff that accomplishes the majority of the work in any given department; target them. Most bureaucracies have a rigid hierarchy, making it also a valid strategy to target the heads of agencies as well. Take care not to invest too heavily in an elected official unless you can be certain of his continued popularity; careful use of other influences can help to insure re-election if properly applied. Barring that, make office holders by appointment your goals. When possessing a measure of control over two or more agencies, be certain to use both to reach a common goal. Left to their own devices, they will almost certainly work at odds with one another. This is the nature of modern bureaucracy.

Cost of Dominance: High to Extremely High. It will not be enough to control the heads of various organizations, or even the mayor. The nature of politics is that one candidate defines herself by disagreeing with others, usually across party lines. Recently human politics has begun to mirror our own, with a sharp division between the established career politicians and the new arrivals to the game. Ironically, it is much easier to gain control of the hungry newcomers than the established powers who have already been purchased. This is not without risk, however. Take care and assess the future viability of any potential political agent; it is an unfortunate reality that job security for these rarely extends beyond a single four-year term.

Any Kindred with either political aspirations or even awareness is almost certain to have at least one contact within the vast governing body of the city. Record these contacts if at all possible, and work to control them. This is a cost effective method of not only the agent, but also what information reaches the ears of specific Kindred. This is the ideal situation, bit also a rare one. It is much more likely that the various agents and contacts will be unknown to you, but will work at odds with your plans. Dominance assumes that you have the collective might to impress your will not only upon the fractious humans, but also on the Kindred or other forces that may be controlling their actions. As with all other areas of interest, dominance requires vigilance on both the human and Kindred forces. There are no constants in politics.

Cost of Neglect: Extremely High. As previously mentioned, a prince who cannot manage the human population in his domain has small chance of ruling the Kindred. So long as no other Kindred dominates, or even comes close to dominion in human politics, you will only be seen as inefficient. This is a major flaw in a public leader, but it is the best of all possible problems should you neglect the political arena. Count on embarrassment. The inability to impress your will and orders upon the city will weaken any foundation you might have otherwise built. Should another possess definitive control of the political climate, you will find yourself hostage to her whim. Awaking in the evening to find your haven condemned is the least of your worries. No prince can ever afford to ignore the political aspects of the kine in his city, and would be well-advised to seek dominion.

Police

Importance: High to Very High. It is the duty of every police officer to maintain order in the city. This works directly in your favor, and puts them easily within the parameters of your vision. The powers of search and seizure are a potent weapon against fellow Kindred and mortals alike, especially as most activity takes place in the sunlight. Arrest warrants may be issued, all points bulletins put out, and suspects held for special interrogation. The police force is an effective citywide army, and it will be used. Be certain that you are one of those utilizing it, lest you be victim of its use.

Cost of Utility: Moderate. It takes very little to make a useful contact with someone in the department; some estimates say that up to 50% of police officers are on the take. Civil servants are notoriously underpaid. It is almost the civic duty of a law and order minded individual to further the cause with a private donation where it will do the most good. It is a small step from eating out of your hand to drinking your blood, and then they're yours. One or two well-placed agents can provide you with the information you need to act effectively. Officers are very good at spotting someone else's strings being pulled, even if they don't know whose or by whom. This alerts you to tampering by other Kindred, and knowledge of a secret is a valuable commodity in our society. They can also provide minor services, such as forwarding copies of files, conveniently losing or rerouting evidence, harassing a malcontent, or even holding a troublesome anarch in an eastern-facing cell until just past dawn. Take care when using your agents, however. Overuse may alert others that they are under your control, and you could lose them. Police work is a very high risk profession.

Cost of Dominance: High. You must control the chief of police as well as precinct and division commanders in order to assure that your orders are followed. It is probable that such total dominion is unlikely in a single human lifetime, and ghouls in service for more than 40 years would attract undue attention. With that in mind, it is advisable to seek out the central administrative arm, the internal affairs division, and either total dominion over either one vital precinct or agents at various levels located throughout the city. It is marginally preferable to have many agents spread throughout the city as more information may be netted, but it is a choice based on personal style and preference. A moderate level of political and media influence will make this a simpler matter, but by no means simple. Possession of the internal affairs division is an advised choice; it offers you the means to neutralize the police agents of other Kindred from within the system. If you manage to achieve this enviable level of control, all that happens within your domain will come to your attention, and you will be in the position to move forces rapidly against whatever threat you wish.

Cost of Neglect: Catastrophic. The situation is similar to neglect of the political arena, only more extreme. Imagine waking to find your businesses raided, your agents imprisoned or fugitives, and your own person the subject of an all points bulletin. All of this and more may befall a prince who does not concern himself with maintaining contact with the civil militia extant in his own city. Unless the prospect of becoming a fugitive in your own domain appeals to you, you cannot afford to neglect the police force.

Summation

The intent of this brief has been to demonstrate the usefulness of various informational sources and human agencies, either to you as prince, or to your enemies should you neglect them. What follows is a prescription for a workable and realistic outline for proper and effective use of these assets attainable in the relative future. Relative future is defined as 20 years or less.

- Computers: Utility.
- Finance: Dominion.
- Nosferatu: Utility.
- Toreador: Utility.
- Media: Dominion.
- Medicine: Utility.
- Government: Utility.
- Police: Utility.

Note that of informational resources, only Finance is recommended to pursue to the level of dominion. You already possess vast wealth; it would be little matter to turn this into even greater, and would take significantly less effort than to achieve a similar level in the others. Avoid the temptation that computer technology presents, for several personal fortunes can be lost on a single ill-conceived idea. Similarly, neither the Nosferatu nor the Toreador are suggested for favoritism. Any such action would have to be in the form of alliances, and an alliance can just as easily become a hindrance rather than an asset. Without knowing the specifics of the clans in your particular city, I could not in good conscience recommend either. Media dominion is vital to a strong and enduring princedom, for with it you can control all public information in regards to the breaking of the Masquerade. Neither the police nor the government are recommended at this time. Should it become necessary to bring members of either agency to heel on individual matters, money and media attention, whether favorable or negative, should be sufficient means by which to achieve your ends.

LINDLY'S
BIG BOOK?
RONALD McBOY
VOL
1
NECRONOMICON
CHEESE
FUN WITH GRAPEFRUIT
VOL 8
ADDITION 4
100000 CAT BREEDS
SPIDER HOLES
HOLY
BRUSHMER '95

A Treatise on Conflict:

How Clan Tremere May Exercise the Greatest Utility from its Enemies.

BY UDOLFO

It is verifiable fact that those on the path of righteousness will be met with resistance from the unenlightened. The wise traveler realizes that every obstacle is an opportunity for gain, however, whether it is personal or for the greater glory of the clan. This will serve as an introductory lesson in the art of conflict management for those who aspire to political greatness.

Enemies Within

Conflict is an undeniable facet of our existence. All of us, whether collectively or as individuals, are constantly seeking gain at the expense of others. Within Kindred society, I shall examine conflict from all perspectives, with an eye to governing the city by arranging enemies against one another.

The Primogen

Traditionally the primogen are comprised of the eldest members of the seven clans. There are a few geographical aberrations, but this definition is sufficiently accepted to stand. These elders are the leaders of the city by default; having survived for centuries, they are powerful beyond the capabilities of the younger Kindred, and thus demand respect. Weak princes rule with permission granted from the primogen, and wise princes consult with them regularly to avoid sedition. Nonetheless, the primogen do not easily set aside the perspectives of their various clans. Indeed, it is much rarer for any consensus to last beyond the duration of any given crisis.

The most powerful members of their clans, the primogen can be an impediment to progress. Each primogen member has the authority and influence to turn her entire clan against the dictates of any other member, even the prince. Therefore, a wise leader will play one against another, keeping himself clear of the fray. For example, there is little love lost between the Toreador and the Nosferatu; the former sees only surface, and the latter sees all too much of the former. It would be a small matter to arrange for members of each clan to spend time with one another. The inevitable will happen, and someone will take umbrage. While the two clans are at one another's metaphorical throats, the prince can take action that one or both would have blocked had they not been preoccupied. Put more plainly, it is wise to cultivate extremity in the primogen, so that there will always be at least one polar opposite to any member on any given issue.

Elders and Anarchs

It is a sad truth that many childer of the other clans do not recognize the superior wisdom of the elders. This is a testament to the foolishly weakening influence of modern egalitarianism so popular among the kine. Many modern childer are either unable or unwilling to abandon the ill-conceived and outmoded ideas of their mortal life and seek a republican ideal for Kindred society. This is not our way, nor shall it ever be. These youngsters are forces of chaos within our society, and they have been labeled anarchs because of this.

The primary mistake these anarchs make is assuming that there are certain natural rights inherent in our existence. This is preposterous; they would not even exist were it not for the beneficence of their sires. Nonetheless, we live in a meritocracy, where the primary merits are patience and continued existence. As the more rash elements wither away, the merits of stability will begin to bear fruit. It is no accident that most elders are cautious and calm.

Despite their disruptive intentions, the anarchs often serve as a unifying force for rational Kindred. By virtue of their own writings and speeches, the anarchs are a threat to our way of life. In light of this, it becomes necessary from time to time to band together and put them again in their proper place. This is the prince's primary function. Internal threats are infinitely more damaging and dangerous than external foes. However, should he prove to be too efficient at this, others may forget his necessity. Therefore, it is often wise to allow the anarchs to gain in strength and number so that they become a threat. After the coalition to destroy them, a period of relatively cooperative peace usually follows in which the various clans at least follow the pretense of working together to further their common interests. Similarly, if the elders among us grow to be too powerful and threaten to unbalance the fragile coalition that allows us to exist, anarchs can be used to divert them. A wise prince would encourage this cyclical growth, allowing first one and then the other to gain power, only to be brought into line by the other.

Interclan strife

Just as the primogen are prone to squabbling, so too are their respective clans. Some of these reasons go back millennia, such as the antipathy between clans Brujah and Ventrue. Others are based on ideological differences or simple aesthetics. Nonetheless, the tension exists. If one can avoid being drawn into it against one's will, it is a force that can at times be harnessed. It is quite similar to organizing strife between the primogen members, only simpler; there are many more individuals involved, more often than not without the benefit of perspective and wisdom that age may bring their elders. Care should be taken, however, not to allow the tension to erupt into full-scale war. Before allowing the strife to escalate, one must be relatively certain one can put an end to it. This is often as simple as calling a meeting of the primogen and explaining to the elders of the warring clans the foolishness of such action in the presence of their contemporaries. Barring this, or if it fails, one should be certain to be able to weather the brief but intense firestorm of street combat. For members of our illustrious clan, such is a simple matter.

Patrician vs. Plebeian

It is the nature of existence that a hierarchy will assert itself in any system, and Kindred are no exception. In regards to social life, there is a marked distinction between those who excel and belong and those who do not. The group of the former is, of course, comprised of the Tremere, the Ventrue and the Toreador. Others from different clans may belong, but this is as rare as one of the above either choosing or being cast out of the upper echelon of social life. Those belonging to the latter group are the Nosferatu, the Brujah, the Malkavians and the Gangrel. Clearly malformed, the Nosferatu have the good grace and discretion to remove themselves from public life. The Malkavians, though often times interesting and insightful creatures, are too unpredictable and unstable to be allowed in proper salons and Elysia on a regular basis. The Gangrel rarely wish to make the social rounds necessary, and the Brujah have nothing but contempt for their betters.

Despite the clear and obvious reasons for the distinction, those of the plebeian caste do not accept their lot with grace, even though their fate was often one of choice. Envy is ever the lot of those who are inferior, and it fuels a seething hatred that can be manipulated. As with interclan strife, however, it is a card that should be infrequently played. Class warfare has destroyed much of the modern world, and continues to do so into the next millennium. It cannot be allowed to do the same for our kind. This form of strife is best suited for our clan to utilize, for we tend to remain withdrawn from social gatherings, even when present. The Ventrue and Toreador, however, are extraordinarily proud of their status, and they will defend it ferociously. If trouble is allowed to occur, it will take little to start it. The Brujah can be depended on for joining in, and the Nosferatu usually cannot resist tormenting the Toreador. This will serve as a rather large and unseemly smoke screen, but it is quite effective in masking whatever large scale action must be taken without the knowledge or interference of the others. Similarly, it is a risky gambit, but reluctant kudos may be offered to one who can form some sort of peace once tempers are allowed to flare and old feuds are rekindled. Due to the nature of risk involved, however, it is not advised; there are other, more stable ways to gain respect and prestige from those reluctant to tender it.

ENEMIES WITHOUT

Though it often seems that we are our own worst enemies, we would be well-advised to remember threats from without. There are many who wish our society ill, be it others of our kind bent on nihilistic perversity, the kine that we so often take for granted, rampaging shapeshifters bent on destruction, or peculiarly talented humans and magi who had not the wisdom to follow us into our current and superior form. Nonetheless, great care should be taken in exercising any of these threats, for none of these enemies have any reason to be trustworthy, much less cooperative. At the very least, Camarilla vampires have the sustenance and survival of our way of life in common. Our external enemies have nothing of the sort to bind them to us.

THE SABBAT

These cretinous vermin are beneath contempt, and should be exterminated whenever possible. This is especially true of the traitorous animals that call themselves Tremere *antitribu*. However, if it is not possible to annihilate them, or if it is not politically feasible, have others do it for you. The Brujah are imminently anxious for combat, and the Sabbat provide an opportunity for violence with little fear of repercussion for any party involved. Even anarchs seem ready to defend their cities from these monsters. No matter who passes away, it is a victory for the Camarilla.

Of more worth than actual Sabbat, and infinitely safer, is the rumor of Sabbat activity. With a known wolf at the door, malcontents are reluctant to weaken anything that may serve as a defense against the greatest threat to the Camarilla way of existence. Care should be taken in manufacturing Sabbat sightings, however, for should they be discovered to be false all future credibility may be lost. More to the point, Kindred may prove reluctant to respond to an actual report. This is much more threatening than any loss of status; Camarilla cities must not fall to these foul beasts. The simplest method of alerting others to the politically expedient threat of a Sabbat incursion is to magnify actual events. Small bands of Kindred, who typically have little or no regard for the Masquerade, are known to roam the outlands and beyond. Whether they are anarchs or the Sabbat, more will respond to accusations of the latter than the former. Do not make the mistake of many princes and elders, however. They accuse all radical Kindred, in particular childer with anarch sympathies, of being Sabbat spies. Unless there is some shred of evidence, avoid this cheap tactic. The bogey man becomes much less threatening if he is invoked too often, particularly for obvious political ends.

KINE

Though simple creatures with no patience or vision, it is unwise to overlook the threat kine bear to our race. The Masquerade is the first Tradition; never forget that. Individually they may prove occasionally enterprising and difficult, yet they are inherently weaker creatures. Nevertheless, they outnumber us by several orders of magnitude, and while it is a simple matter to dispatch one, or even several, few of us could survive a mob, much less worldwide exposure. The latter is the gravest danger they pose. Be aware of this when using kine against one's enemies.

The safest and most effective use of humans is to mercilessly harry one's enemies. When dealing with individuals or officials of order (police officers, utility workers, government officials and private investigators) the primary fear any Kindred should have is that of the Masquerade. This fear of exposure, combined with possessing many secrets that the Kindred wishes to remain hidden, will make for a very effective and unnerving encounter. Several such encounters in rapid succession will unravel even the most resolute elder. Some have been known to vacate cities in response to just such harassment. Note that I do not speak of ghouls and other retainers, who have been brought into our world and society by virtue of the knowledge that we exist. Any who cannot use such readily available tools is beyond instruction.

SHAPESHIFTERS

These creatures are individually more dangerous than the Sabbat. As we are to humans, so are they to us. What knowledge has been gleaned from survived encounters with this race of homicidal proteans has led to the conclusion that they bear us an irrational, religious hatred that can only be satiated with our total destruction. Unfortunately, we lack the might to demand a compromise as was done with the Assamites. The cities are our domains, the wilderness theirs. Great care should be taken with any attempt to use these creatures against one's enemies, for they are holy warriors against us who are as likely to kill both the target and he who requested the assassination. Yet they do serve a very real purpose in the maintenance of order.

Because it is known that they roam the wild areas between enclaves of civilization, intercity traffic of our kind is extremely limited. This is true to such an extent that it is relatively easy to track all who enter or leave, and it fosters a sense of siege mentality, particularly when the Lupines have attacked in recent memory. They make a very serviceable sword of Damocles, encouraging others to work together when otherwise they would not. Fortunately, it appears that these shape shifters are more occupied with internal strife and other concerns to turn their full attention to us, an eventuality that should chill the blood of any Kindred.

MAGI AND OTHER MYTHIC CREATURES

It appears that the forces of magic are returning to the world, if reports are to be believed. Humans are again casting cantrips, sometimes with startlingly efficient results. Reports, all from reputable witnesses, have also registered such creatures as satyrs, demons, ghosts and wyrms. If at all possible, avoid these, for they wield powers unknown to us, and have a range of motility beyond our own nocturnal cycles. In particular, take extreme care in the presence of human magi, and report any such contact immediately to your superiors.

Even rumor can serve, however. Activities can be masked as undertakings by these classes of beings, especially if the imagination has been sown with rumors and phenomena beforehand.

Little is more gratifying than witnessing one's enemies run themselves into exhaustion while attempting to find an enemy that does not exist. Fortune will surely smile upon you of they do indeed run afoul of the creatures they believe to be at fault, for carnage will most likely ensue and your enemoies will be ill-equipped to defend against unknown powers.

This treatise has been general by design, hoping more to set the mind at work, rather than provide a blueprint to be copied wholesale. There is no such adversity, except perhaps the final death, which cannot be turned into an asset. If no other lesson is to be learned than this alone, all has not been in vain.

In the service of the greater glory of Clan Tremere,
Udolfo

M E M O

Jean,

As requested by Monsieur P., here is my general analysis of the clans and their probable reactions to the ascension of a new prince. It would seem to be a simple matter to extrapolate the reactions to a proposed king, as well; increase the negative by the same order of magnitude that the positive is decreased. Again, I urge Monsieur P. caution; time will in no way diminish the validity of his claims.

Michel

On the Leading of the Clans

Kindred society is much like a synthesis of the medieval guild system and the aristocracy of Europe until the early 20th century. Power and influence are grouped according to membership in a familially structured group known as the clan. These clans are not lineages in any standard sense, but more a collection of individuals infected with identical viruses that are, with minor exceptions, identical to the viruses of the other clan groups. It is around these differences, however, that family groups are formed. The delineation of the virus and its wide scale morphological and behavioral effects are the subject of another inquiry. Only those aspects pertinent to the discussion of the political and social structure of the Kindred shall be addressed herein.

Traditional history, both oral and written, classifies Kindred into 13 groupings, each named after a mythic, historically suspect sire or dam, reflecting the adolescent desire for validation and the tidy answer to the teleologically troubling question of existence. That each sire or dam traces lineage back to the biblical Caine [*sic*] is a clear example of the internalization of persecution, namely that the afflicted are indeed terrifying predators cursed to be the eternal "other." The similarities to social and political outcasts among humanity, the "unafflicted," are clear. What we are left with is a society that is comprised of individuals who expend a great deal of self-definitional effort in setting themselves apart, attempting to come together on the basis of similarity. It is little wonder that Kindred society is notoriously unstable.

What follows is an analysis of the seven tribe groups that comprise the majority of the Camarilla and their responses to and views on the institute of princedom. In their dealings with one another, the tribe groups cluster to what they perceive as like, recreating the aristocratic hierarchy common throughout much of history. As political definitions, the Brujah, Gangrel, Malkavian and Nosferatu clans make up the "lower four," while the Toreador, Tremere and Ventrue comprise the "upper three." To speak broadly about familial and cultural groups among humans would be extremely prejudicial, and reflect more of the speaker's perspective than any meaningful observation concerning the subject. To speak so of Kindred groups is significantly less prejudicial; one is not "born" into a clan, but is chosen to join. Such choice is usually based upon a degree of sympathy between the infector and the infected.

Brujah

These Kindred are bound together primarily by their rebellious nature, a nature that is only increased by the most marked behavioral symptom of vampirism. They are quick to anger, and particularly well-equipped to give expression to it. Violence is most often the preferred means of discourse. Individually or as a group, they are iconoclastic. It is little surprise that the vast majority of the anarchs come from this clan.

Any hierarchical system of government is by definition discriminatory. Power in a closed system is limited; those with it wish to accumulate more at the expense of those with less. In Kindred society, it skews heavily toward the eldest, in a system not unlike other strongly filial societies. The Brujah are political dilettantes, riding the wave of whatever ideology is prominent among humanity. As this is the modern, postmonarchical age in the West, it should come as little surprise that this clan heavily favors a republican or democratic form of government, as opposed to the institutional despotism that has been the norm for centuries among our kind. It is a small matter to lure members of this clan to the sides of change and revolt, but it is much more difficult to form any sustainable coalition with them once power has been attained. The failure of the soviet experiment demonstrates their instability even when they alone are in charge.

If seeking to recruit members of this clan, approach their elders with respect. A degree of personal bravado is expected as well. Do not treat them as the leather clad hooligans their childer often are; many of these elders are quite literate and well informed. Present arguments in a direct manner, but do not expect them to go unchallenged; this is not a clan of followers. If you can make a favorable showing in debate, you may gain the respect of the elders. This is a much simpler and more elegant way than demonstrating physical superiority to the gang-like packs of young Brujah who seem content with turf warfare and an arbitrary system of renown based on daring and combat. Take care to stress the role of clan advisors and the role of the primogen. Choose terms that allude to council based government. Above all, give them something other than yourself to rebel against.

What do we want? Only something you'll never give: freedom. Eternity isn't about kissing butt and being a toady, it's about either making it or failing on your own merits. But then I guess you wouldn't understand that, would you? All princes are going to fall sooner or later because there are more of us than there are of them, and we're gaining more every day. The tyrants today, the smooth talkers tomorrow, and the "benign" despots at the end. Of course, if they're really benign, they'll see that we're right....

Gangrel

Of all the tribe groups, these are the most independent, solitary and self-reliant. They insist on defining themselves as a collection of individuals, and never as a cohesive unit. If the Brujah are pack minded, the Gangrel are solitary nomads. Like many other nomadic societies, they have a long-established oral tradition. When two or more Gangrel meet, it will be an evening of long stories, relating personal observations and hearsay. If one Gangrel speaks well of you, it will soon pass to others through this method.

The Gangrel value their autonomy above all else. It is unspoken tradition to allow them free entry into and exit from all Camarilla cities, and with good reason. Well-disposed, they are a source of information from other cities and the outlands where most of our kind fear to venture. Angered, they are individually some of the most combat-capable Kindred to be found. If many are angered, even Brujah give them wide berth. Secondarily, they are intensely concerned with nature and justice, the former most often in collusion with the latter. Their sense of justice is powerful, though often biblical in its harshness.

The simplest manner of avoiding their wrath is to be just when dealing with them. They do not often care for politics or intrigue; do not bring them into it against their will. If they can be convinced of injustices originating from an extant administration, they may temporarily join in opposing it. Most Gangrel have little truck with princes, and they prefer to keep it that way. Do not force them to take notice of you.

What do the Gangrel want? This Gangrel just wants to be left alone for the most part. I come and go as I please because I'm not afraid of what lies outside the cities. Sit in them and scheme for all I care, but don't drag me into it. Remember that I go where you're afraid to go, and deal with what you're afraid to deal with, damn near every night. Think hard about that.

Malkavian

Similar to the Brujah, these Kindred are also deeply affected by vampirism behaviorally. Unlike the Brujah, however, who share a common mental affliction, the Malkavians each suffer from a unique affliction not unlike those found in humanity. While actual numbers of the human "insane" are still being debated, it can be assumed that significantly less than the majority possess those negative mental states that those in power deem dangerous to social order. With these Kindred, all are marked aberrations from the joint construct of sanity. Members of this clan work together with deceptive ease in spite of (or perhaps because of) their differing mental perspectives. Many Kindred ignore Malkavians, only to fall victim to elaborate pranks that demonstrate a frightening degree of personal knowledge concerning their person and habits. Insanity is a shroud of incredible use.

Regarding the institute of princedom, Malkavians do not speak with a unified voice. Some number as anarchs, and some are staunchly conservative. Often one will find individuals from either extreme of the political spectrum sharing pleasant conversation; compartmentalization of differences seems to be a common asset. A common mistake in dealing with Malkavians is persecuting the entire clan for a collection of minor inconveniences and annoyances. Nothing will mobilize the most persecuted of clans against a prince faster than a blanket accusation against them. Deal with each as an individual, and inform elders of action against members of their clan. Even a modicum of gentility and respect, if not perceived as condescension, may earn good will. Avoid persecution, discourage it from others, and aside from the occasional disturbance, you should expect no trouble from this clan.

So the turtle has come to the cuckoo, has she? How interesting...What does the king of all she surveys wish of this little gnat? Oh, the princedom. I've often found that many are only 10 or 11 inches; they fall short. Be sure you're all 12, and the first step is realizing that you can't do it alone. There are powers larger than yourself that you have to consider. But then why should you listen to me? No one else listens to the little man in the refrigerator who works so hard to keep the light on when it should be on and off when it should be off. Maybe you know better than they, eh?

Nosferatu

As a class, none are more readily discernible than the Nosferatu. Each is warped by the process of change, clearly marking their lineage. Their abilities at obfuscation, both visually and informationally, can be seen as a blessing, allowing them to disguise the marks of their "affliction." However, there is a growing movement to deny the necessity of hiding their visages from other Kindred. The direction and degree of cultural transference in the idea of reclaiming words and ideas that were previously prejudicial and culturally harmful is an interesting question; are riot grrrls, "queers" and racial minorities following the example of their comrades in oppression, or have the Nosferatu appropriated human cultural ideas and implemented them? Whatever the origin, this clan possesses a sense of unity that is one based on visual commonality and negative value assigned their "curse." They are a tight-knit group who have excelled — much like Jewish businessmen in Moorish domain — in areas that others are loath to explore. The Nosferatu have long been the forerunners among Kindred society in shifting to the information economy; the trade of secrets has been their domain for centuries, whereas humanity has only begun in the past several decades the wholesale shift to this medium. With the rapid development in communication technology, both are advancing at an ever accelerating rate.

As information brokers, it is vital to have a good business relationship with the Nosferatu. This is the very least. Better still is to have them for allies, though they do not give their loyalty lightly or cheaply. One point that is fundamental in dealing with them is that of domain. Centuries of precedent have established the Second Tradition to apply to the prince and the princedom, yet the Nosferatu claim the sewers as their own. Grant this, for it is a small thing to give, yet the price for withholding it is incalculable. The prospect of an invisible cadre of spies working diligently and efficiently against you should give substantial pause. Treat them as equals, though it may dismay members of the self-styled ruling elite clans. Centuries of abuse and discrimination have made them suspicious of kindness. Be persistent, for just as they are slow to grant their loyalty, they are similarly slow to discard it. Though it should never come to an exclusive situation, I would advise extremely careful consideration of the worth of the totality of the "upper three" versus the Nosferatu alone.

Ya wanna know things? Ya came to the right place, then. Most folks do, sooner or later, at least the smart ones. Take a seat. Yeah, that really is a chair... prince, huh? They're the ones who paint this big design of concentric red an' white circles all over themselves. I never understood the point, but I'm no fashion expert. Huh, you didn't take the bait. Anyway, they're the ones that try to run things, only most bite off a lot more than they can chew. Just 'cause they have a title doesn't mean they can do stuff, especially not unilaterally. It takes good information to make good decisions. I can see you're one of the ones that get this simple but vital point. Now let's talk about price....

Toreador

Beauty is the curse and blessing of this clan. The vampiric condition engenders a capacity for a fugue-like appreciation or absorption with the beautiful that is the well-known and often mocked weakness of the Toreador. (Despite the Romantic connotations, no reference to *toro* or to Spanish origin are part of the oral and written tradition of these Kindred.) This is the precondition for their obsession with art, or the wholesale rejection of it. These reactions, properties of the artiste and poseur cliques respectively, reenact the classic attempts to gain some form of control over that which dominates the individual. It is nothing more than working within the "system," or rejecting it wholesale.

Toreador are social creatures. They often behave as *nouveau riche* striving to master the salon culture they believe to be their duty, much like the subjects of television melodramas. They have internalized an aesthetic of their elders, most without considering the benefits and restrictions.

The opposite extreme is that of the tortured artist, the Byronic hero who must suffer for his art in an attempt to recreate as a capricious muse the petty tyrant that controls his perceptions. Despite their position on the polaric scale, all Toreador are primarily concerned with beauty and the artificial attempt to create it. Politically, they seek protection for and access to these works and the environments that create them. Any alliance with them must take these factors into consideration. You do more than your political aspirations a favor by virtue of patronage, but you must take care not to patronize one artist, medium, or locale to such an extent as to slight others. The Toreador are quite sensitive to slight, whether intentional or perceptual. If at all possible, portray the previous or extant prince as indifferent or antagonistic to the arts. This task should be a relatively simple matter, as most princes are more consumed with the nightly operation of their domain than with the status of a particular artist. Take pains not to fall victim to this yourself. If the previous prince was known as a patron, the best you can hope for is that the Toreador will not take sides in the political arena. If they do, they will stand with the known patron.

Obviously, we want some degree of safety, but not stifling control. How can art flourish when rigidity is the norm? There is no art then, only clever rendering. There must be some degree of risk in the air, some feeling that anything could happen. Creativity demands no less. Of course, we do not wish for street warfare or Machiavellian backbiting: tres passé. Wit, however...do not confuse feeble scheming for true wit, for only a fool sees no difference. Which reminds me, did you hear what a certain highly placed Ventrue said at the opera last night...?

Tremere

Despite the shroud of archaic mystery and hermetism, the Tremere are by definition the most modern of all the clans. Unlike the other clans, there is no inherent flaw specific to the Tremere as a result of the vampiric condition. Nor is there a mythic, pre-Cambrian progenitor and creation myth. Their founder is extant, if reclusive. If their claims are to be believed, the initial ranks of the Tremere were chosen from the ranks of literate, analytical natural scientists of their day. Certainly not devoid of any superstition themselves, one cannot help but wonder if their act of self-creation, distinctly separate from the others, has freed them from the instinctually supported myth. All restraint and limitation are derived from social structure, and are clearly recognized as constructs.

The Tremere are a reclusive and mysterious clan, and wish to remain so. Rumors of dark and sinister experiments constantly surround this clan; do not investigate them too thoroughly, lest you earn their enmity. Allow them their secrets, until so doing becomes politically untenable, or until they transgress the traditions. Politically conservative, they favor order over all else. Should you be able to make substantive progress toward stability, if not nominal peace, the Tremere should support you. If, however, you wish to unseat a competent, though stifling prince, they will ally against you, preferring the known to the unknown if it is beyond their control. Be very wary of accepting gifts or aid from them; the Tremere are well-known for their ability to offer proper assistance at critical moments. Though it may prove to be useful, even vital, the eventual price for such aid will be commensurate to this value. Once in power, the Tremere will support you so long as the Masquerade is maintained. Be wary of angering them, for though your organization may survive their antipathy, it will likely not survive their enmity.

Order is of primary importance to Clan Tremere. None of us are safe if the Masquerade is broken. Discipline is paramount; those in charge cannot afford the luxury of compassion. Leave that for mortals. Our way requires more. What we seek in a prince is the ability to see our society as a collective, a whole, rather than a collection of fractious and vocal individuals. If few must be cast aside so that the safety of the rest are assured, then so be it. Naturally, the most violent and chaotic among us would be the logical choice for such an act of selfless sacrifice. Never let it be said that the anarchs are wholly without merit.

Ventrue

Exclusivity personified, or perhaps vilified. Though the changes wrought by vampirism in members of this clan have been debated as being both physical and behavioral, more recent inquiries focus on the mental aspect, specifically internalization. The ruling classes throughout history have been known for discrimination, whether genuine or affected. In the Ventrue, this discrimination has reached its ultimate peak: the ability to ingest only certain blood from certain individuals. Curiously, there is no pattern to this exclusivity save what might be gleaned from a deep knowledge of the particular Ventrue. Most are aware of this, and guard themselves against any true degree of closeness lest their individual weakness be disclosed. This level of caution borders on the paranoid; it is as if each member of this clan, known to frequently fill leadership positions, assumes the distance that is common between true leaders and their flock.

This personal distance manifests as a conservatism that surpasses any in either human or Kindred not of the Ventrue clan. This extends to both the personal and the institutional. Members are accustomed to positions of supremacy, in particular the trappings that often accompany such positions. Wealth is synonymous with security, and it is flaunted with unconscious ease as the one visible distinction between the aristocracy and the commoners. This penchant for the cautious approach and plodding pace of achievement makes recruitment of these Kindred a difficult task. No action will be taken unless it is clear that the chances for success far outstrip the possibility of failure; Ventrue are not known as gamblers or risk takers. Cast careful and precise plans, outline each contingency, and Ventrue will listen. Tradition, as well as the Traditions, are of paramount importance to this clan. Be certain to make yourself more appealing on these grounds than the previous prince. If, as will most likely be the case, the predecessor was a Ventrue, expect only slightly more resistance from this clan. Each member harbors a secret belief that he or she would be a better ruler than any other, and has a personal list of flaws and mistakes that known sovereign have made. Appeal to the existence of this list without making specific reference to it. Revealing too great a degree of personal knowledge about a member of this clan will be met with instant suspicion bordering on the pathological. Once in a position of leadership, patience and care are the keys to dealing with the Ventrue. The anticipation of perceived flaws implies the correction and avoidance of them. Above all else, do not appear as rash and headstrong. Work to secure the safety of the Ventrue, and they will follow.

A prince should be many things: a shining example of noblesse oblige, a savvy negotiator, a ruthless and efficient enforcer of our laws, and a careful strategist with deep knowledge of current and future trends. These criteria are nonnegotiable, having been proven necessary and sufficient over the centuries. Decorum is only slightly less important, but its lacking may be overlooked if it is not too great and the other requirements are met. Of course, most Ventrue worthy of that name possess all of these traits, and were chosen to join our ranks on the basis of their closeness to this ideal. We typically rule cities for a reason, you know.

It is my hope, Monsieur P., that this treatise may serve your needs. Knowledge of the clans, the particulars of the vampiric state that define them as tribe groups, and how these particular traits have been dealt with historically, gives a significant amount of information about the outlook of each. A careful approach, based on this knowledge and couched in terms to appeal to the intended target, would increase your chances of success. However, let me urge caution in this matter. Patience has ever been a virtue of your line, with the few exceptions serving as a warning in their failure. Allow the organization to grow slowly until such time as all agents can combine their power and expertise to achieve your ends. The goal itself is noble; I would be more loath to see it fail than my personal involvement alone could account for.

As ever, I am yours to command.

M. F.

THE FOLLOWING PAGES WERE
FOUND IN THE PERSONAL
EFFECTS OF LODIN, LATE
PRINCE OF CHICAGO.
HANDWRITTEN ON AGED
PARCHMENT, THEY WERE
OBVIOUSLY QUITE OLD AND
WELL CARED FOR, THOUGH
THE CRACKED LEATHER
FOLIO THAT PROTECTED THEM
APPEARED TO HAVE BEEN
SCORCHED BY FIRE.

K.M.G.

Well, Maxwell,

It seems that you have finally attained the position that you sought for so long. I'm certain that your ears are ringing with the congratulations of your contemporaries. Fear not, this shall not add to their number.

I realize that the transition is a busy time, and that you have many enemies to pursue and critics to silence in the days ahead. However, it is my hope that you will take the time to listen at the knee of one who has made the mistakes he cautions you against.

Despite what the more ambitious Kindred advisors may tell you, the actual running of a city is easy. If you can attain the position by virtue of anything other than sheer luck, then you have already established a model for the nightly operation of your prize. Forget for the moment clan strife, the antipathy between elders and their progeny, or even the Sabbat; any moderately competent administrator can discern ways to deal with these problems. Instead, I shall define three arenas in which it is vital to establish your dominance: the public, the personal and the private.

The Public Face

It has been called many things: the persona, the facade and countless others. The public face is something that most wear, though few ever shape it to meet their needs. This is the arena that most usually associate with a prince. As a leader who wishes to survive for any length of time, you cannot afford the luxuries of apathy and indifference. Only fools or clever enemies will tell you that honesty is the best policy; the former out of ignorance or naiveté, and the latter out of an active desire to do you ill.

You must shape the face that you present to all. You have been developing the raw materials for such an endeavor since your first duplicitous act. Take stock of what you possess, and do not be afraid to discard that which no longer serves. Do not be hasty in this, Maxwell; patience has never been one of your virtues. Think of it, then, as brooding; you were ever one for that. Regardless, you must consider all options.

Take, for instance, your optimism. I know, you thought you had hidden it in the guise of idealism, and for some this may have been effective, but not for me. Rest assured that if I can see it, others can as well. They will use it as a hook, appealing to your dream of a better life, and that will prove to be your undoing. Never, ever present anyone with a true weakness. This is not the same as presenting a front devoid of any weakness; that will only arouse suspicion and unwanted curiosity. Do not be seamless, no matter how hard you present yourself. Riddles beg to be solved, so you must be certain to have several artificial solutions prepared.

Perhaps these generalities are confusing. Let me offer an example: Let us suppose that a relatively new prince has come to power, and he is quite naive politically. Furthermore, he truly wishes to believe the best about others, despite the lessons to the contrary that experience and time have provided. Finally, there is a dream of a perfect city, so vast and overpowering that it threatens to consume his soul. I am sure you will agree that it is not much to work with, but it serves for my purposes.

The first weakness is relatively simple to disguise. Naiveté is an unfortunately common vice, but it need not be fatal. An acceptable response when confronted with a question that you might be incapable of dealing with — or not willing to deal with — is silence, punctuated with either a steely glare or seeming indifference. As the silence stretches, the supplicant should become uncomfortable. Let the silence grow again by half past what you think is sufficient, then ask the presenter of the problem how he would suggest that you deal with it. If executed correctly, this ploy will shift the weight of the situation from your shoulders to his, for he will assume that he presented you with information that you already possess, and that you are now testing his suggested answer. Take note, Maxwell; everyone has secrets that weigh heavily on their consciences.

If you foster the impression that you possess more knowledge than you actually do, they will become fearful, and go to great lengths to cover their sins. If you are particularly astute, you may gain leverage on the supplicant who unwisely overprotects himself in a given area. Rest assured, it is there that his secret lies, unless he is more adept at this game than you. Never forget that possibility.

As for wishing to believe the best of others, this is a severe flaw in anyone who would wish to survive among our kind. I cannot stress this enough to you. I can see two causes for such a dire handicap: laziness and stupidity. Laziness is by far the more dangerous reason, for it is an underlying flaw that will permeate all that you do. Do not convince yourself that others pose you no threat simply because you do not wish to properly prepare yourself against them. This is a luxury that few of our kind may indulge in, yet none who attains a position of dominance can harbor this frailty and long survive. You must assume that all have reason to wish you ill. In political terms, a friend is someone who sees no profit in becoming your enemy at this time. Investigate your contemporaries thoroughly. Discover what they value, what they hate, and who sets themselves with and against them. Take a lesson from the lunatics, and try to place yourself inside their minds. Think as they think, plot as

... interes ... rbing trend in rec... ...over the ... ...es. ...rce, if any, will come to dominate Austin. Our agents have had but lit... forecasting the city's political climate.

A closer look at Los Angeles confirms that the anarchs are a danger to the Camarilla. On the other hand, the Anarch Free State is definitely going to be a short-lived problem. Chaos is the rule here, and the Masquerade is broken nightly. The defacto leaders are already grumbling about having to cover up the mistakes of others. Soon they will have more in common with the elders of Camarilla cities than with their revolutionary comrades. This is what happens when you try to build upon a dream alone. Without structure and experience, this experiment will fail. My prediction is 20 years at most.

THE CIRCLE QUARTERLY

they plot. If your information is accurate, you may gain invaluable insight. If, on the other hand, you are a smiling dolt who cannot conceive of malice in others, I am certain that the more pragmatic of our kind will do you the kind favor of removing you from the stage of politics. They will also most likely remove your head as well. Remember, Maxwell, that there are few ex-princes, yet there are many dead ones.

Now to the obsession, the vision of the perfect city that our hypothetical prince is accosted by. All leaders of merit must possess vision; without it they are nothing more than a bark in a tempest, being moved in various directions by forces beyond their control. Many so-called princes end up following this course, having become more concerned with maintaining their position than with accomplishing anything of worth. These are not leaders, but figureheads. You shall not become one of their number. I will correct this mistake personally if need be. I trust you recall what a harsh teacher I can be.

Worse than lack of vision, however, is blindness. Those who strive to straddle fences to retain their gilded thrones are at least aware of the shifting forces around them; they must be. Zealots are not so bound to the realities of our existence. They see naught but the perfect world of their vision, and are consequently incapable of timely or effective action. Our exemplary prince suffers from just such a malady. He seeks to recreate the glorious cities of antiquity, which is certainly a noble goal. However, our prince is so blinded by his dream that he sees and can think of little else. Both perception and reaction are based not on actual circumstances, but on an ideal which does not exist. Wearing such fetters, our prince cannot be proactive to any real event. The best that he can hope for is to be manipulated by those who are aware of his dream. The worst he can expect is death.

Clearly the wise prince would fall between these two extremes. It is a sad truth that wise princes are exceedingly rare. One finds in their place petty despots and paranoid bureaucrats. Our prince should combine the political savvy of those who are only concerned with maintenance and the dedication of the zealots. He should take wisdom from the ancients: Moderation in all things.

Crafting the Facade

Now that our prince has realistic flaws, let us consider his strengths. These shall serve as the skeleton of the persona that we shall shape for him. Let us presume in him a tenacity equal to the wolverine indigenous to your new home. He shall also possess a strength of will and an active nature that, when used in concert, proves to be quite effective. He shall be a learned man, a product of continental culture with an acute and insightful awareness of history. Finally, let us assume he is of a scholarly breed with a past so long and glorious that few can recall it, and only see him as an aimless nomad, or at best an itinerant dreamer. These are not inconsequential merits, and can prove to be an effective foundation.

Anticipate the reactions of others, Maxwell. Place yourself in the position of our fictitious prince, a task most certainly not beyond you. You should depend on being misperceived; it is your one-time advantage in dealing with others. They will expect a tempestuous dilettante or fiery ideologue. Never be what others expect of you, unless it serves your purpose. Others may be lulled into complacency by the proper presentation of their own expectation. Our prince might gain the freedom to observe and scheme without being observed himself if he plays the part of the short tempered dilettante, yet he must be aware of what he loses in the bargain. It has been my experience that it is much easier to return to type having presented an unexpected face, rather than vice versa.

Your purpose is to unbalance your potential enemies. You would be well-advised to consider all who visit you as such. Do not overlook mortal prejudices in this matter. If your contemporaries still insist on seeing you as an inferior merely due to the continent of your ancestry, they will have crafted a hurdle for themselves that you must exploit. Blood knows no color, nor does it know gender. If they expect inconstancy, offer them stability. Play upon your education and your grasp of culture. Offer them not a spartan war room, but a civilized parlor. Be polite, especially when they are expecting abruptness or anger. To return to our prince, he would be well-advised to display himself as one well cultured, even tempered and polite. Others will see him as either an aberration, a break from his kin, or as constructing an elaborate front to hide something. If observers assume the first, all the better: The best one can hope for is to be underestimated. Unfortunately, most will assume the latter. It is to them that I address my next point.

No matter how carefully you may construct your persona, it will be pierced. Expect this, and prepare for it. A lie is best concealed by another lie. You must have another persona ready, one that "rings true" to your audience. Your primary public persona, assuming you are in a similar situation to our fictitious prince, is one that plays against

Helena,

I wouldn't worry too much about Dorfman's interview with Vitel. Dorfman is either a complete idiot or an incredibly savvy politician. Apparently, all it takes is a smile and being treated slightly better than a cockroach to convince your pontifex that what Marcus says is true. No new information changed hands, really. Marcus gave a seemingly sincere apology about the death of Phelps, and promises to look into it. His new line is that the Giovanni are in town again. Dorfman seemed eager to chase that old whipping dog again, though he tried hard to hide it. What a fool! There has been no Giovanni activity in the D.C. area for years. I'd guess he's itching for a chance to learn the alleged secrets of death. Hmm…perhaps a frame job, brought to the attention of his superiors, might be beneficial to your position. Just idle speculation on my part, though if it bears fruit, I am sure you will remember the one who gave you the seed.

M.B.

expectations. Therefore, your secondary persona should be more in line with what you assume they wish to see. Show them the wrathful, frustrated idealist who is quick to anger. The best lies are the ones that both play to expectations and contain a kernel of truth. Be careful, however, to avoid showing interest or anger toward things that truly matter to you. Under no circumstances should our prince let his zeal for the ideal city be known. Instead, let him show a propensity to lingering vendettas over minor slights and a penchant for action. Anarchy should be suppressed, and its proponents offer a wonderful opportunity for cautionary harshness to those who would oppose him. He should not hesitate to take physical action himself when there is little to be lost. Additionally, the occasional lapse into personal violence can be refreshing, clearing the mind of all save the immediacy of the experience. I am certain you know of what I speak.

Having now two personae, our prince need only work them both to his best advantage. Were he wise, he would portray the primary persona, that of the cultured, well-bred gentleman, as the thin veneer of civilization covering the petty, violent despot he usually pretends to be. All that remains concerning public performance is the shifting between the two. Again, it is not wise to show a featureless, impregnable wall. The secondary persona should be allowed to "slip." Be certain to take note of those who show no surprise; they are the ones who are already planning to manipulate you by way of your exposed weakness. The one true point to be made here is that you cannot become predictable. This extends to the shifting between personae. If you have been far too restrained, fly into a rage over the slightest offense. If you have been brooding and violent, a prospect not difficult to imagine with you, swallow your pride, exercise your will, and refuse to be baited by obvious insults and challenges. Of course, all of this is applicable to more than two personae, but that is perhaps too advanced for you now, Maxwell. Begin slowly, and do not make mistakes.

The Personal Face

Remember all that you have been told about the public persona and apply it to all situations where you wish to distance yourself from your most public face. Do not fool yourself into believing that you can remove all masks among any of our kind, for we are a vicious breed, and we will turn on any weakness that presents itself. Perhaps not today, but eventually, the adder in your breast will strike. Yet no prince can rule from the balcony alone. There is no surer way to insurrection than an eternally distant liege. I will now tell you how to avoid this occurrence.

Just as you need a public persona, you also need one for private audiences. A private audience is any situation in which you wish to foster the impression among those present that you are lessening the distance between you, that you are revealing a confidence. This can even be the confidence of a direct threat or show of anger. It need not be an act reserved for an audience of one.

It will not suffice to merely revamp your public persona for personal use. No measure of trust will be gained from presenting your audience with that which you freely offer to others; it must be something new. This is something that you have done many times before. I am positive that you do not reveal your true motivations to those with whom you speak. Your continued existence is proof of this. This time, your advantage will be that you consciously craft this mask prior to its use. I seem to recall your wits being incapable of fabricating a convincing act at the scene of the crime.

Let us return to our prince, who has been a fine example thus far. As you will recall, his aim is to convince others that he is showing a truer face. He will find that it is easier to convince someone of his authenticity if he exists within a known frame of reference. No matter that he can converse fluently in five languages and lecture on the art and science of the Florentine Duomo, the primary persona of a man of culture and learning will not be comfortable to many simply because it is so contrary to their expectations. This is especially true of our brethren who are most often known for art, commerce and occult trafficking. Consequently, he must move to meet them on their ground in this. He must make concessions to their prejudices in order to convince them of his sincerity. I am sure that our fictitious prince would be amused at the irony of misleading those conceited aristocrats by way of their own bigotry.

Similarly, the petty despot, though much closer to stereotype, is too uncomfortable for easy toleration. Despite — or perhaps because of — the prejudices our prince will face due to his lineage, none of his subjects truly wishes to see him as the quintessential sanguinary insurgent. It is useful to note that those who are most strongly prejudiced are also those who cannot stand to have an "inferior" in a position of power over them. If our prince wishes to retain his position, he should in some way allay the fears of his detractors and present a less violent face in personal situations. The obvious choice for a private persona would be an amalgam of the primary and secondary public faces, rather than a construct that is uniquely whole and distinct from either.

Our prince should blend the worldliness and culture of his person with the passionate temperament of his lineage to create a believable persona. There is the possibility that these are the traits that the prince himself possesses, at least in part. This is commendable; the acting is easier to sustain if some part of the role is also a part of the actor. Take note of our prince, however. He is careful not to carelessly reveal as his own passions the passions of the role, nor the inverse. He is eminently aware of the relative ease in blurring his own motivations with those of this facade because it is so much closer to his own true nature. You in particular should learn from this creation of a prince.

Let us return to the lessons learned in dealing with your public. Again, one facade will not be enough, nor should it. You must create personae to fit your needs. A careful actor would try to root each in some aspect of himself. A careful prince would go further and have at least some recognizable link to a previously established persona. Not only does this provide continuity, but it reduces your work considerably. Though I understand that you wish to do things in the most difficult way imaginable, Maxwell, you need not reinvent the wheel every time you ride in a carriage. You may think that I am asking you to reflect on every word, motion and tone of voice in every social situation, and you would be correct. The spotlight serves to illumine you, to serve as a targeting beacon. You must be prepared if you wish to endure and prosper. Though the entire senate took part in the murder of Caesar, one knife alone would have sufficed. Lower your guard at your own peril.

The Private Self

I have told you how to deal with others. Now I will tell you how to deal with your truest and most clever enemy: yourself. Forget for the moment all acting and assumption of roles; this is anathema to self-knowledge. The prince who misleads his subjects is wise. The prince who misleads himself is a fool. You carry the seeds to your own destruction within your breast. I do not speak in metaphor here, Maxwell. I speak of our primal nature, the howling savage who lurks just below the surface. It is particularly strong in you, a combination of your passionate nature that sets you apart from the rest of the common herd so many years ago, and my own familial influence. In regards to this Beast I can offer you few words of advice, for each must forge his own way with it. Do not be tempted by it. Though it offers power and simplicity, this purity of existence is not without considerable cost. I do not think that you are truly willing to forsake all claim to your position, nor all social interaction beyond violence and the search for sustenance. Understand that which drives this primitive heart. It wishes for security and dominance, desires that strike a resonant chord with the desire to rule over others. Channel this energy to your own ends, for it has been my experience that the Beast can be mollified when its needs are met. In simpler terms, being a successful prince may be the proper prescription. Many of the virtues of leadership are also a tonic to this internal hazard.

It can be said without doubt that you are ambitious. Were you not, there would be no need for this correspondence, for I would not be lecturing you on these matters. Take care, however, that the Beast within does not disguise its actions and motivations as mere ambition. Become aware of the possibility, and turn it to your advantage. You wish to create something uniquely your own, a domain wherein you shall live in safety and comfort. The Beast also wishes for this. How convenient for you that the Traditions that rule us also serve your purpose. Does not the ruler of a city have the power to allocate its finite resources? It is not unheard of for a prince to reserve the choicest livestock and hunting grounds for himself, and few would expect anything less of you. Properly fed, your primitive aspect will not concern itself with fear of scarcity.

As a leader, you are held accountable for the safety of all within your domain. Much can be done in the name of safety; protecting yourself can easily be explained as protecting others. It is merely a question of redefinition. Anything that is a personal danger to you cannot be presented as such. Instead, it is called a danger to the entire domain. Political turmoil serves as a fine example. Unless, as prince, you have succeeded in alienating a significant number of your subjects, most will not wish to risk themselves for political motivation. It is much more difficult to overthrow an institution than to work within it when it offers protection from enemies. Under the guise of protecting your realm, protect yourself. Do not be afraid of being ruthless, but neither should you fear the appearance of mercy. If forced to choose between clemency and harshness, you should always choose the latter. If you are too harsh with an individual, the odds are quite good that he will not be available to seek redress. On the other hand, if you are too lenient, your mistakes will return to haunt you. The lesson to be learned is that by guarding your domain, you also guard against your darker half. Manage your affairs, lest the Beast manage you.

Pay heed to what I will next tell you, Maxwell: Restrain your temper. This is the crack through which the more active and capable of our kind fall prey to the Beast. With care you can procure enough sustenance and create a level of safety that will hold it in check. There is little proof against anger. Your fury, much like my own, is legendary. Do not think that your enemies are unaware of this, for they are already planning to exploit this weakness. One need know nothing more than your lineage to possess knowledge of this weakness, for weakness it most certainly is. There is a time for righteous anger, yet when the howling Beast obscures all with scarlet fury, it is difficult to be discriminate in your wrath. You must hold it in check; your will is for nothing if not for this. Do not be manipulated by your heritage.

Having addressed the Beast, let me now address the oft overlooked aspect of your state: your human emotions. Forget not from whence you come, Maxwell. Though you are a breed apart, you still share much with the common mass of humanity. The history of human existence is written in its own blood. That which is assigned negative worth, namely fear, hatred and desire, has already been discussed. Your nature merely exacerbates these. Yet there is also another aspect to emotional life that you would do well to acknowledge.

Having considered and dealt with vice, I will address virtue. I shall not speak of religious tenets.

The demands of your existence make such exhortations shallow condescension. Leaving dogma and ethics behind, I will tell you something of the values and dangers of compassion, remorse and love.

You already know much about ruthlessness, compassion's opposite. I have told you to be hard when necessary, and I do not retract this. Ruthlessness is for your subjects to witness and tremble. Compassion is for you alone. Allow me to explain. Compassion is generally seen in two lights: the feeling of sympathy for those who are suffering, and the desire to alleviate that suffering. You cannot afford to deny these feelings. In the short term, pure ruthlessness can be a great asset. Yet we do not exist in the short term, and cannot afford to think in terms of anything less than generations. The road of pure power, devoid of compassion, leads directly into the arms of the ravening Beast. It is ironic that the quest for control of one's domain so often leads to loss of control of one's self, yet that is the nature of our existence. However, frequent displays of compassion will limit your effectiveness as a leader. At best, your displays of emotion will be questioned. At worst, they will be believed, and your resolve and steadiness will be questioned. Compassion, especially sincere compassion, is a luxury a prince cannot often display in public. To put things simply, you must feel sympathy for those in pain lest you descend to an animalistic state of brutishness, yet you cannot publicly act on this sympathy. Kings often have private confessors and numerous confidants. Princes have no such luxury, nor can they afford it. You will be alone with this pain and you will anguish over it. When it threatens to overwhelm you, take solace in the fact that it is better than the alternative. It may well be the only comfort you have.

Remorse is perilously close to compassion, yet still not the most dangerous and necessary of emotions. While compassion deals with pain and suffering in general, remorse applies specifically to those you feel you have wronged. Do not forget my injunctions against self-delusion; a prince who convinces himself that he has truly wronged none quickly becomes cold and hard, but will eventually become brittle and rigid. Neither of these traits are found in successful, or even long-lived princes. Political necessity aside, you will wrong others, many if you hold your position for any appreciable length of time. Do not ignore these pangs of conscience, for in doing so, you again approach the savage within. Much like compassion, you cannot afford to make a show of suffering the injustices you heap upon others. You must feel this, yet you cannot share it with any. If you must act, do so long after the deed has transpired, and act in so mysterious a manner that none will see your motivation as what it is and seize upon it as a weakness. Reward a childe if you have punished her sire. Offer boons and rewards that give the appearance of furthering your own agenda: grant exclusive hunting rights with the injunction to police the area and restrain others from breaking our traditions therein; allow an elder to adopt as a childe one whom you wish to see join our ranks. Also, do not forget the world of the common herd; great suffering can be alleviated with but a minor exercise of your powers and influences, and such a nonspecific act of charity may mollify your guilt. Though not pure by any stretch of the imagination, these are the only public acts of remorse you can afford. Remorse, too, is often a public liability in a ruler, yet it is a necessity in one of our kind.

Love: Never has more blood been spilt nor more redemption found than because of this emotion. Unless you are significantly more degenerate than I am aware of, you will still be susceptible to its call. This is not in itself a weakness: far from it. You cannot ignore the realities of your situation or station, however. We are a cruel, predatory breed, more often than not concerned about our own survival over all else. It is a sad truth of life that love is rarely reciprocal, and virtually never in exact proportions. These vagaries are troubling enough in commoners, yet they invite disaster in our kind. One is never so vulnerable as when one has totally exposed oneself to the object of ardor. In the best of all possible situations, nothing is more rewarding than requited love, and nothing keeps the darkness further at bay. Should this lucky occurrence befall you, however, understand the potential liability a consort may be seen as. Do not attempt to disguise the situation; make it abundantly clear. Make no missteps, but punish fiercely and finally any who would use the object of your affections to your detriment. For once, your dark half would seek the same ends I would encourage you to take. Love — true love — is a rare gift. Do not make the mistake of many who only realize its worth once it is no longer in their possession.

As I have said, however, true love is rare, especially among our kind. It is much more common for there to be some discrepancy of emotional intensity between the pursuer and the pursued. If you find yourself in the position of the pursued, no matter how unlikely (unless things are much different in the New World than on the Continent), you should capitalize on the situation. Courtship is a game; study Capellanus if you do not recall the rules. Do not hesitate to make demands on your pursuer, demands that will serve your own ends. If you are the pursuer, rest assured that the object of your affections will most certainly do the same to you. I would advise you to court only those for whom you feel no strong emotion. You will still gain the prestige of courtship, and it will pass the time in a moderately pleasant manner. If you are strongly smitten, however, do nothing at first but observe. Above all else, you do not want to draw undue attention to your interest in the observed. I am certain you can imagine the leverage one might try to gain with such knowledge. Exercise your critical facilities to the utmost, and strive to remain objective. I would advise you not to initiate any action on your own, but I realize that such advice will most likely go unheeded in the heat of passion. Instead, I will urge caution. Make no move that is unabashedly motivated by love; rather, encourage the object of affection to make a similar move. Under no circumstances, however, should you engage in any bonding of your pursued to yourself. Such action provides the mere illusion of love; its steadiness and unwavering nature only add to the knowledge of its unnatural origin. Take this opportunity to learn from the mistakes of another; the death of one who was once loved is a difficult burden to bear, infinitely more so when the beloved was slain by your own hands. If the choice is to merely pine or bond the beloved, I strongly encourage you to be satisfied with pining; much great literature has arisen from similar circumstances.

You must walk a very narrow path. You must be firm, resolute and enigmatic to your public, yet you cannot afford to become cold and hard in actuality. You must feel the pain of those who you wrong, yet you must not become maudlin and ineffectual because of these emotions. You will feel the desire for love, yet you must not expose yourself or your beloved to your enemies. In essence, you must remain a vibrant and feeling individual, yet show little or none of these emotions to others; you must lead a compartmentalized life, alone with your emotions and hard pressed to find appropriate expression for them. Such is the nature of princedom. It is a decidedly solitary existence, yet one which cannot be abdicated without great personal risk. It is the proverbial tiger; once grasped, it cannot be safely loosed. It is my hope that, with my advice and your own natural intelligence, you will come to accords with the tiger, and serve it as much as it serves you. Do not believe that you can control it, and do not let it control you. It is my instruction to rule well and long. Do not disappoint me, Maxwell.

Estefan

A Manifesto on Becoming Prince

I am going to tell you how to become the prince of a city.
The elders who claim the right to control us by their more
potent blood would see me destroyed for what I am about to
tell you. You may not believe me, but a letter such as this,
were it to fall into the right hands, is capable of causing
more damage than an entire army of anarchs could to those
decrepit fools. Those who rule do not share their secrets;
those who attain power and who are wise do not reveal how
they achieved their position. I am telling you these things
because in you I see a power worth cultivating; a leader
capable of becoming a dynamic prince in whatever city you
choose as your domain. I am writing this to tell you about
those tactics that I have found to be effective in that long
climb to the top. Heed my advice, and you will prosper. Ignore it, and think of me when they stake you out for sunrise.

You may be asking yourself who I am. What city do I rule
over that I should dare to give such advice? I am no prince.
I rule over no domain, nor shall I ever. If I did, I would
see this letter suppressed and destroyed. I have fought the
elders for centuries, since before the betrayal of the Council of Thorns.

I remember the day of the great betrayal, even as my
fellow soldiers shackled themselves with a few strokes of the
pen. I was the only one among us to really see the fear behind the elders' eyes, and secure in that knowledge, I walked
forth from that chamber with my head held high....

On those first nights after the great betrayal, the elders
were faced with a very real threat to their security. Those
anarchs who chose to submit to the Convention were Blood
Bound to the elders of the fledgling Camarilla, their punish-
ment to slave for their new masters as the front line of
defense in preserving their precious Masquerade. Today many
of those ex-anarchs who survived are the princes and primogen
of many cities. This shall be my revenge upon them: I shall
help those who are now younger, hungrier and most ambitious
to take the power that was given in return for this traitorous service. My only payment for the secrets I give you is
your success, for it means that some traitor whom I have
known for five centuries has seen his last sunset.

As for what I shall tell you, the elders do not want these
things to be known. I have, in my long years, seen many attempts at seizing the title of prince. Some have even
succeeded. I have seen which tactics work, and what mistakes
are commonly made. I have fought the elders of our kind for
centuries, and my vengeance upon them is to tell you, who
still covets their position, how to supplant them.

As for what you do once you have seated yourself on your throne, I care not. It is the bodies that you will inevitably step over to reach that throne that interest me.

I. On Establishing a Mortal Power Base.

The first step in your quest for dominance among Kindred is to build a power base from mortals. This is easier said than done. We revel in our ability to control and manipulate that which is around us. This is not to say that we are submissive to authority ourselves — the Brujah and the anarchs are proof of this — but we all desire some control over our existence. We want secured feeding grounds, enough status to give us the freedom to pursue our pleasures, and the security to be able to hide from our enemies. It does not matter what ideology one follows, we Kindred are self interested creatures, and our primary goal is perpetuating our own survival.

The best way that we Kindred have of assuring our survival is to control the resources of mortal society. Unlike the mortals, who see the world as full of endless resources free for the taking, we Kindred see the world as a dark place with very scarce resources worth killing, but not dying for. Our primary purpose lies in establishing safe and reliable herds, and this is only possible through controlling those things that keep the kine strong and secure. As a result, all sensible Kindred establish control over an area that they will guard against all comers. This territory, whether it is a physical area, an aspect of Kindred political life, or some area of mortal influence, will be that Kindred's own personal domain. All Kindred attempt to build such domains, and they jealously guard their holdings.

Because of this brutal fact of Kindred society, you will find that every aspect of whatever city you have chosen to make as your home has some amount of Kindred influence over it already. As such, you will find yourself in a very interesting situation. Namely, you will only be able to increase your influence at the expense of another. This is yet another reality of our kind. The only way that you will succeed is through another's failure. The only way that we Kindred can gain some stability or security is by taking it from another. This is the primary reason why friendships are impossible among our kind. We are the quintessential predators, and in the end, we will feed upon each other.

Your first priority in building a base of influence over mortal society is to achieve financial stability. Just how you get the money that will be necessary for you to expand your influence is up to you, but remember that you must pay your bills before you can take over the city. Do not laugh. I have seen a single audit destroy some Kindred. I have watched creditors chase a Cainite across a half-dozen new identities, ignorant of what they pursued but willing to brave the gates of Hell to retrieve their assets. You must acquire assets that are both extensive and secure. This is the primary reason that so many of us fake our deaths after the Embrace, or go to great lengths to establish new identities. It secures our liquid assets so that even our beloved heirs cannot get their hands on them.

Once you have established yourself as financially stable and are able to raise some funds, your next priority will be to make some long-term investments. Anything that you choose to put your money into over a period of time counts as such. You may want to make traditional investments — I recommend utilities or real estate — or you may simply choose to put your money into very tangible assets, such as houses, cars and other property which can be turned into cash with a minimum of fuss. It is a very good idea to make sure that these items are in someone else's name, preferably that of a Blood Bound ghoul who will not only minister your affairs but also remember to pay the property taxes.

Always remember that in whatever you do, the Ventrue will have been there first, and that you are treading in their domain. They will have bigger houses, faster cars and more powerful businesses under their sway. Do not let this bother you. Remember, you are not in competition with them just yet. So long as you do not present a threat to them, the blue bloods will ignore you in their arrogance. Just remember to tread carefully and avoid stepping on any toes until you're at the point where you can do so with spikes on your soles.

Your next priority will be to establish some police ties for yourself. Once again, you will find that other Cainites have been here long before you. It will be safe to assume that in any Camarilla-held city most commissioners, precinct heads and other upper echelon police officers are controlled by the ruling prince or powerful elders. It will also not be unusual for most neonates to have occasional beat cops conditioned to look the other way concerning their feeding habits. With just about every Kindred in the city interested in controlling some aspect of the police, you will find that your priority will be to find some niche in the city's law enforcement which you can lock all other Kindred out of. This will involve identifying which aspects of the police force are most open to exploitation and subversion. Internal Affairs is ideal, but is rarely available. However, any department has dents in its armor.

The most important thing to remember is that any police department is made up of people, and people have weaknesses. It doesn't matter how you establish control over a faction of the police department, just make sure that your control is solid and firm. Once you have even one small aspect of a police department under your control, you can begin to widen the scope of your influence. If you have even one policeman under your sway, work hard to get him promoted and then subvert his subordinates as well. Then start pushing for transfers for your people to other precincts. This way, whole precinct houses can be under your command in relatively little time.

In any city the traditional news media (television, newspapers, radio, etc.) will be controlled by the elders. Nothing is more crucial to the preservation of the Masquerade than the literal control of what the kine see. Since these elders will have such tight control over these sources of information, they will be especially vigilant about their property. Stay away from the traditional media until you have grown strong indeed, or else you will attract unwanted attention from above before you are ready to handle it.

Instead, concentrate on the less traditional and new media of communication. The sad truth about the elders is that they are very slow to understand the potential of new technologies. As such, they are constantly letting tools of infinite promise slip right by them. By the time they realize the impact that, say, the Internet has on society, it will be too late for subtlety. They will react in their typical manner, buying their way in, establishing control and attempting to manipulate the content of that medium of communication. At that point it is already too late: The message they had hoped to stifle has already been broadcast.

In most cases, those oh-so-subtle manipulations of the elders will be noticed by the kine, many of whom will perceive the media in question as having "sold out" or "gone commercial." The result is that the elders will find the audience that they have just purchased moving on to other, more "cutting-edge" technologies. So find and seize these new media wherever you can. Concerts, performances and Web sites are all virgin territory for our kind, and they present the perfect opportunity to scurry around the cordon of silence that your elders have created. Play your cards right and you will soon be able to extend almost unbelievable influence over the kine. I do not jest; you will affect how they think. Your primary goal so far as the media is concerned is in finding new types media and encouraging their growth in the directions you desire. There is reason to be careful here as

well. You will not run into elders online, but you may well
run into the neonates and ancillae whom they control. They
will have just as much knowledge and interest in these media
sources as you, and a master to please as well.

In any case,you should not have too much trouble gaining
influence over the underground and nontraditional methods of
communication in your city. You may even wish to start your
own. Now that you have a voice, you can expose all of your
enemies' breaches of the Masquerade (or, if you can't find
any violations, make up your own. Who says you have to play
fair?) You can then turn around and use your influence to
cover up those breaks in the Masquerade and curry favors from
the grateful elders.

1. Organized Crime

In every city, there is some form of organized crime.
Criminal activity has existed since the beginning of time,
and organizing it simply makes it more profitable. Crime has
low overhead, high profitability and marvelous fringe benefits. It yields money, weapons and willing soldiers which
can be used to expand your influence among both mortals and
the Jyhad. It is no wonder that so many other Cainites attempt to control and manipulate this one aspect of mortal
society.

Achieving control over the criminal element in the city
you are in will be tricky, but not impossible. The criminal
underworld is composed of many different elements, from
street gangs to insider trading flacks. What you must do is
simply pick one selection from the buffet of wrongdoing and
concentrate on that, rather than attempting to swallow the
whole thing at once. If, on the other hand, you try a little
of this and a little of that, someone else will steal the
contents of each main dish out from under you, leaving you
with scraps.

You will find it very difficult to work your way into the
organized crime networks in a city. Every faction of Kindred
society has its finger in the criminal pie. Elders and
Ventrue concentrate on organized syndicates and white-collar
crime, money laundering and fraud. Anarchs counter by controlling the gangs on the streets, and their retainers mug
those of the Ventrue. Delving further into the depths, one
finds that the Giovanni have been the most successful at
establishing control over "traditional" crime families, while
the Followers of Set have the most success at controlling the
worldwide drug trade. If you choose to expand your influence
into organized crime, be aware of the players involved. Information is key here. Know whose territory you will be

infringing upon and scout out their weaknesses before making
even the first move in their direction. Otherwise, you will
never gain so much as a toehold before being squashed.

The key to controlling the underworld is twofold. The
first thing that is necessary is for you to either establish
or take over a hierarchical crime network. Place into this
hierarchy trusted retainers and give them enough autonomy so
that they feel as if they are benefiting themselves as much
as you. The one beautiful aspect of organized crime is that a
well-maintained organization runs itself. Once a criminal
network has been established, it regulates itself. Your only
priority is to ensure loyalty, which you can do by occasionally showing the iron fist inside your velvet glove. Run your
organization as ruthlessly as possible, but reward lavishly
those who serve you well. When properly applied, the stick
and carrot are all that you need. Your organization will do
most of your work for you, making you a force to be reckoned
with without your raising more than the occasional finger.

The second aspect of controlling the underworld in your
chosen city will be to encourage and assist the anarchs in
gaining power over the gangs that they do not already dominate. Do not dirty your hands yourself by getting involved
with this aspect of the underworld. Instead, make inroads
with the anarchs and let them recruit your bully boys for
you. Portray yourself to the anarchs as a patron. Make them
think that their little gang empires are a personal power
base. If you play your cards right, larger and larger pieces
of the pie will find their way onto your plate.

2. Civil Bureaucracy

Being able to control or manipulate information and data
is very powerful, and being able to get the location of a
rival's haven by looking up his utility bill is very useful.
Government is extremely difficult to infiltrate, as everyone
wants a piece of it, but once you're in, the benefits are
magnificent.

3. Churches and Religious Organizations

This is a dubious area in which to establish an influence.
For many Kindred, it is enough simply to be able to use the
sway held over organized religion to prevent the Society of
Leopold from coming to town. There are some Ventrue who see
many of the televangelists and their shows as potential cash
cows, and such Kindred will infiltrate and control these
organizations simply to skim as much money as they can from
them. On the other hand, while televangelists are rarely
troubled by faith, their parishioners often are. This can
lead to nasty surprises.

The best reason to get a televangelist or charismatic preacher in your fold is for the slave-like obedience he will likely be able to extract from his followers. This can be translated into protests, votes and other useful toys.

4. Health

The advantages of this are obvious: blood in easy-to-carry bags and convenient places to store corpses. More than one Kindred of my acquaintance has found that a morgue makes a wonderful haven if you don't care much about ambiance.

5. High Society

This is the domain of the truly blue-blooded — the most powerful and most glamorous people in any given area. The people who are the controlling interest in the public aspects of the city are the intelligentsia, the art patrons, the old money elite and the political families. Many of these people have their own considerable resources to call upon, and should you bend them to your will, you will have those resources as well. Often ambitious Kindred think this will be one of the best places to gain a foothold. Too bad the Ventrue and Toreador have beat you to it. Instead, wait until the control of another area gives you an entry into the world of martinis and Martha's Vineyard beach houses, then move as quickly as you can.

6. Industry

While this may bring up images of smokestacks and factories, this also includes access to the technologies that those very same industries are producing. Controlling or getting access to new technologies is an advantage that you should always press. The elders locked away in their Elysiums have no idea what the kine is capable of today, or if they do they have deluded themselves into believing that they are safe from the power of silicon and split atoms. I want to see an elder stand up to a hydrogen bomb. I really do.

7. The Legal System

Establishing a presence here could involve anything from simply having a few lawyers at your beck and call to having established a network of judges and courts under your heel. Being able to sue your enemy may not seem to be a very effective way to take on another Kindred, but what about a 2:00 PM court date ? You may also want to consider the haven-breaking power inherent in search warrants and zoning regulations.

8. Occult

Controlling the shadowy culture of occultism and mysticism in the world of darkness will allow the smart Kindred access to incredible amounts of forbidden lore. Of course, it will also yield an almost unending parade of yahoos. Walk softly, as the Tremere have harvested here first.

9. The "Street"

Think of it as disorganized crime. By the "street," I mean lower echelon gang members, prostitutes, beggars, petty criminals, etc. These are the legions of mostly forgotten kine who inhabit the darkest parts of the lands of the living. For all of their failures, these folks have developed an incredible tenacity. They are a superb source of information, and useful tools for dirty work as well. Keeping your hands in this area will at least keep you appraised of what is going on behind the scenes in a given city. Respect the territory of the Nosferatu who has inevitably been here before you, and you will tap into an information network nearly as comprehensive as that of the Sewer Rats.

Transportation: Depending on the city, this could be one of the most important areas of influence around. If a city is isolated, control over who or what enters and leaves is very important. A Kindred can use such control to monitor other Kindred's comings and goings. An area can become isolated or may only be opened up to your allies.

10. Education

This is perhaps one of the most insidious ways to subvert a reigning prince's rule. After all, every prince is watching to see if the city government or the police are being subverted, but the school system? A university? Attack is less likely from that direction, so vigilance is weak. Besides, if you have time to wait, remember that the ghoul you make in the schoolyard today will be a policeman in 10 years, a lawyer in 15 or a mayor in 30....

II. Alliances, Form and Function

It is a simple task to establish yourself in mortal society. It is much more difficult to establish yourself among the Kindred. We are social creatures, but then again, we are also inherently cannibalistic. In every aspect of Kindred society, there are secret unwritten rules of conduct that determine our status. Oh, we hold to the Traditions, never forget that; but beneath the Traditions there is no law in Kindred society save that which we make for ourselves. Just make certain you know whose rules you are playing by and you will prosper. On the other hand, the rules of the anarchs and the elders are quite different, and if you find yourself in the wrong game you'll be snuffed out like a candle.

You will need to make alliances with different groups within Kindred society in order to secure your own status, and to have a firm base of political support when you make your move. Remember that an alliance can take any form, from an informal agreement between yourself and a Nosferatu trash picker to an intricately written treaty between two factions.

You have the responsibility to uphold your end of such an alliance no matter what, even if your putative allies choose to back out or betray you. If nothing else, you must portray yourself as honorable and trustworthy. This will benefit you for two reasons: First, if you can get the Harpies on your side, they will be certain to damage those who have betrayed you or failed to live up to their end of the bargain as long as they can sympathize with the poor betrayed, and second, when you do chose to break your word or betray your allies (and you should only do these things in the most dire of circumstances) they will be caught completely by surprise.

This is not to say that you should allow others to play you for a patsy, or to blindly enter into alliances with other Kindred. Remember that you must always uphold your end of the bargain, and if they have failed to fulfill their terms, crush them. Do this, not for vengeance's sake, but as a reminder to anyone else who is thinking of reneging on a deal.

Remember that within Kindred society, how you are perceived is infinitely more important than how you truly are. You must decide what you want other Kindred to perceive as your goals and motivations. Once you know what image you want to project, do all that you can to insure that all Kindred in the city know who you are. Are you the righteous avenger, constantly fighting against the current prince's injustices and gathering your forces for the grand fight? Are you the territorial loner, controlling everything you hold sway over with an iron fist and crushing those who cross you? Or are you a quiet and dignified clan member, serving your fellow Kindred and simply staying neutral in the affairs of the city? How you portray yourself will be essential to how the other Kindred in the city approach you and deal with you, and will dictate the types of alliance others approach you to form.

<u>Types of Alliances</u>

1. All for One...

Often these alliances are based upon a group of Kindred who are all pursuing a common goal, whether it is a group of anarchs that have banded together to diabolize an elder or a band of ancillae creating an intricately worded treaty that details sharing resources to approve funding for a housing project. In these coteries, it is often very simple to get someone back in line who may be thinking of backing out. Just tell them to remember "the cause," and they will inevitably come running back because of intense feelings of guilt.

2. Enemy

A group of Kindred may choose to band together to destroy a common enemy. This type of alliance can be counted on to last until the enemy in question is dead and no sooner, though some have lasted quite some time as the members discover imminent threat after imminent threat. Some of these coteries end up as roving hunter-killer gangs and they usually find themselves put down for their own good.

3. Protection

Perhaps the prince has become too oppressive as of late, or perhaps the Sabbat are attacking the city. In any case, a group of Kindred often choose to ally against a threat until it has passed. While there's nothing wrong with creative cowardice, these types of alliances do have one weakness: They are extremely simple to exploit. Shout, "The Antediluvians are coming! Run!" and watch them scurry.

4. Influence

A group of Kindred often decides that rather than fighting, they can exploit the resources of a city together. As such, they can merge their organizations, establishing unprecedented influence over the city. These inevitably last until one member of the central committee decides that her partners are getting a better deal than she is. At this point, things tend to fall apart in a shower of diablerie. On the other hand, a partner can be useful in your ascent — up to a point.

5. Information

This is one of the least formal, and most common types of alliances. It consists of a group of Kindred who simply keep each other informed of current events. The advantage of this type of alliance is that it can be used to gather incredible

amounts of information with a minimal expenditure of resources. The disadvantage is that it can just as easily be
used to spread misinformation or outright lies, and it's
damned near impossible to track the source of the misinformation. Of course, if you are the one spreading rumors, this
isn't such a disadvantage.

III. Politics After Sundown

The various groups within Kindred society have differing
goals, strengths and weaknesses. Any Kindred who would attempt to make his mark, especially as a prince, must
understand how to approach these different groups. I will not
say that our many little groups of Kindred fall neatly into
stereotypes — that would make them all far too easy to exploit, after all — but many do seem to fall into hoary
behavior patterns. Those patterns can be studied, learned and
— if you do not fall into them yourself — exploited.

1. Brujah

If you oppose authority, then you are their brother. If
you find this to be the case, encourage familiarity with
them. Lead them, but do not rule over them. They will chafe
against any authority, even self-imposed. Never bully them,
but if someone else has been foolish enough to do so, then
make a show of striking back. Do this, and you shall gain
their respect. Gain their respect and they will follow you to
the gates of hell, shouting your slogan all the way.

What you may offer them: Offer to the Brujah the tools of
the fight: guns, blood, feeding grounds and political protection. Give them the opportunity to rebuild their little
Carthage, and constantly let them know that you support their
plans to reestablish Carthage within the Camarilla. Give them
catchy phrases like "Death to tyrants, even dead ones!" and
so forth; phrases like that are easy for them to remember.

What you must expect from them: Expect arguments. Expect
defiance. The Brujah, while they may be fighters, are not
soldiers. They do not subscribe well to a military mentality,
preferring the tactics of the mob. Instead, your best course
of action is to find out what goals the Brujah have, find
ways to convince the Rabble that their goals will best be
served with you in charge, and turn them loose.

2. Gangrel

These Kindred are more territorial than any other Kindred.
They often lay claim to some desolate wilderness area and
then challenge any and all who enter. The biggest mistake
that you can make is to trespass in their domain. Let the
prince do that instead.

When you approach the Gangrel, make sure that you respect their customs and their traditions. Many of their ways may seem alien or downright barbaric to others, but they do have a certain vigor. The Gangrel in the city (those few who stick around) tend to be a neutral and individualistic lot. They are also very honest and straightforward (at least to each other). Do whatever you can to gain their respect. Once you have their respect you will have more aid than you can possibly imagine.

What you can offer them: Whatever they want. Those things that the Gangrel tend to want are things like Kindred staying out of city parks or for some logging company to be shut down. Put this in perspective; compared to the scope of the Jyhad, what does this cost you? Give it to them. Remember, however, that the mere fact that you have bribed them does not mean that they will fight for you.

What you can expect from them: The Gangrel will not pay attention to you. By virtue of many years of betrayal, they will be mistrustful. Worst of all, they treat all other Kindred as the rest of us treat the Ventrue. Vow not to lose your temper with their attitude and things will be much easier for you.

3. Malkavians

There is absolutely no discernible pattern of behavior to these lunatics. They share no common interests, no common goals and no discernible hierarchy that may be bargained with. Some of the Malkavians make excellent allies, some make terrible enemies and some make a good meal.

What you can offer them: There is nothing that you can offer to the Malkavians as a gestalt. Find out what each one wants, then give it to them. Or don't. Patience truly is a virtue when dealing with the madmen of our kind.

What you can expect from them: Are you jesting? There is nothing that you can expect from a Malkavian. Remember that when a Malkavian makes his move, no matter how extensively you have prepared, you will *not* be ready for what happens.

4. Nosferatu

When you approach this clan, you must not show that you are offended by their appearance no matter how hard they will try to make you pull back in revulsion. They will respond favorably to you if you approach them as equals and treat them as you would any other Kindred. This will impress the Nosferatu as to your character, but do not think it will ever earn their trust. The Nosferatu are suspicious of all other Kindred, and few will involve themselves overtly in politics. They are concerned with practical things, and they value

isolation more than anything else. You will never be seen as
an equal by the Nosferatu, so gaining their friendship will
be impossible.

As an aside, I recommend meeting with Nosferatu on neutral
ground. The sewers have swallowed up more than one would-be
prince, while you certainly don't want them in your haven,
dripping slime on the carpet (and memorizing both location
and entry points).

What you may offer them: What could you possibly offer
when they control all of the information in the city? They
will want favors, not material goods, and the price will be
high. However, it will be more than worth it, I assure you.
If it helps, think of it as a long-term investment in the
city. Buy the prince's secrets from them, and pay whatever
they ask — once. Offering them the freedom to develop and
expand their underground domains may win you friends. On the
other hand, permission matters little to their kind.

What you may expect from them: They will be telling you
the truth, unless the prince has paid them off. In that case,
they will be lying to you. They also will be telling the
prince the truth, unless you have paid them off, in which
case they will be lying to him. Remember this: They are spying on you, too.

5. The Toreador

You are entering dangerous territory when you deal with
this clan, notorious for some of the most bitter infighting
in Kindred society. The Toreador are split between their two
factions — the Artistes and the Poseurs — and as they're not
actually fighting over anything important, they reach new
heights of viciousness. The Artistes control the most prestige within the clan, and therefore they are the most valued
and respected elders in Toreador eyes only. The Poseurs, on
the other hand, are masters at Kindred politics and the games
of presentation and intrigue that the elders play. In almost
any city, the leader of the Harpies is a Toreador Poseur. If
you can get the Harpies on your side, you will become politically unstoppable.

What you can offer them: Praise them. Go to their parties.
Appeal to their vanity and their sense of culture. Go to
their art shows. Do not act rudely toward a Toreador, unless
you are doing it deliberately to amuse another degenerate.
Demonstrate your command, and do not allow any of your co-
horts to be rude to them. If someone has slighted the
Toreador, you may attempt to curry the favor of the Toreador
by publicly humiliating the offending party at a later date.
This is not only useful, but also enjoyable, if I may say so
myself.

What you may expect from them: They will offer you political advice scattered between the catty remarks. Heed their warnings, as they are masters of intrigue and have played the same political games for centuries. A warning: Any advice that they give you will also be in their own interest. They will always side with their clan above all else. If they offer help, do not refuse, as many Toreador have resources to call upon that make some Ventrue green with envy.

6. Tremere

Dealing with any Tremere is an invitation to trouble. Arrogant and vicious, the Tremere have a tendency to use and manipulate others out of sheer habit. They are very dangerous adversaries, but are even more dangerous as allies. The Warlocks have a nasty habit of running off, licking their wounds, and then coming back and incinerating those who have displeased them.

Capitalize on the fact that nobody trusts them, so either force them to work toward your ends or keep them so busy watching their own backs that they can't hurl daggers at yours. Tell others that the Tremere must have been up to something and feel free to make up the details of the plot. No matter how *outré* the one you come up with may be, rest assured, they've probably been up to something even stranger. A final note: Find out where the Chantry is. The real one.

What you can offer them: If you must deal with the Tremere, offer them favors. Only deal with the Tremere if you know that you can claw your way out of the meeting if you must. Never accept anything from the Tremere unless you know what you must give in return. Never accept a boon from them unless in the most dire of straits. If at all possible, on the other hand, put yourself in a position to offer them favors and don't wait for them to act to extend your services.

What you can expect from them: The Tremere will use and manipulate you at every opportunity. They will never show their internal dissension to the others — it is unheard of. That is not to say that the Tremere do not fight each other, simply that they don't do it when the children are watching, if you catch my drift. If you find yourself witness to an internal Tremere dispute, side with the Chantry leader. The Chantry leader *always* wins.

7. Ventrue

The Ventrue will have more money, more status, more power, more influence and more contacts then you do. Deal with it. They have enough resources to buy and sell most other Kindred 10 times over. With the exception of the prince's brood, every Ventrue secretly wants to be the prince. They want the power and the prestige, and they feel that they will have the power to fight their so-called "secret masters." Keep this in mind when you deal with the Ventrue: They are such subtle manipulators that their paranoia makes them feel that they are constantly being subtly manipulated.

What you can offer them: When they have everything? The only thing that you can offer the Ventrue is the opportunity to achieve more power and influence in the city. In fact, your best bet is to make them think that they are manipulating you. Be careful, though. The Ventrue play hard. When the time comes, kill as many as you can, especially those Ventrue who were your closest allies. After all, they're seeing you as a useful way to achieve power for themselves.

What you can expect from them: They will never side with a non-Ventrue. They truly do see themselves as separate from — and in some ways superior to — all other Kindred. This arrogance can be used against them, for it makes them pathetically predictable.

Other Clans

1. Assamites

Hire them first. More important than hiring them as assassins is contracting them as bodyguards, if you have the resources. Many Kindred do not realize just how valuable Assamites are as guards. Always be honest with them. They will never side with non-Assamites against their own, but you can always buy them off, or at least prevent your enemies from hiring them.

2. Followers of Set

Never, ever, ever: talk to them, listen to them, accept any favors from them, pay attention to them or even think about them unless you are about to kill them.

3. Giovanni

Dealing with these Kindred is very much like dealing with the Devil himself. The Giovanni look out only for themselves. You can hope for very little from them. They prefer not to bother with Kindred politics, instead relying on their influence over mortal society and knowledge of the realms of the dead. Do not enlist the help the Giovanni if you can avoid it; if you are not careful, you may find yourself quite literally selling your soul to them. If you must deal with the Necromancers, offer them a fair deal, with both sides getting their cut up front. Never borrow money from them.

4. Ravnos

Never trust a Ravnos. Watch over all of your possessions when they are even within shouting distance. Use whatever position that you have in the city to encourage the prince to step on these vagabonds, but make certain that your name is not attached to the deed. If you can get away with it, frame them for anything that you have done. If a Ravnos takes something from you, leave it be, no matter how important the item in question might be to you. If you tempted a Ravnos by telling her how important the trinket was to you, you deserved to lose it.

5. Anarchs

As a whole, the anarchs are petty and stupid thugs. Offer them the petty things that petty men want. Offer them blood, feeding grounds, guns, etc. All that you can expect from the anarchs is stupidity and a comfortable place to stop a bullet. They spend most of their time in their "Anarch Councils" trying to crush the elders with the same predictable tactics, rhetoric and dogma, year after year. The anarchs are nothing but pawns, and if they are not your pawns, they will be someone else's. Remember that is rare for a pawn to checkmate a king, but enough of them can be a threat to lesser pieces — like you.

The Sects

1. The Sabbat

If you have ever considered joining the Sabbat, then I urge you to make your choice now and hold yourself to whatever decision you make. Waffling won't make it any easier. I was tempted to join the Sabbat in its halcyon early days, but in the end I came to the decision that the Sabbat is not much different from the Camarilla at its core. The elders are still just as powerful and manipulative; only now they don't have to pretend to be civil.

All Sabbat vampires whom you encounter will almost inevitably be nastier, stronger and fiercer than you. You may wonder what advantage you would have against such creatures. It is this: No matter how much an elder hates and fears you, he will hate and fear the Sabbat more. The best course of action for you is to rely on your ability to deal with and relate to others. When the Sabbat enter the city, sit back and let the prince and cronies take care of it (and send the Harpies after the prince if he doesn't). If you are lucky, you might wind up rid of both. If you must deal with the

Sabbat, offer them anything — the chance to commit Diablerie
on prince and primogen, the opportunity to make some new
recruits, the moon in a hatbox — whatever it takes. Just make
sure that whatever deal you cut does not allow them to remain in the city once they've served your purpose. Grant them
not a single square inch. Once the Sabbat have established a
foothold in your city, you are doomed.

2. The Inconnu

I know nothing of these ancients. They are all powerful
and are not to be trifled with, but consider concerns like
yours to be beneath their notice. They lurk in the shadows
and watch the rest of us for any signs of the coming Gehenna.
Unless you stumble across one in her lair, Inconnu are no
threat. If you avoid them, they will avoid you. If you find
that you must fight against one of them, I can recommend to
you a lawyer who specializes in wills and the like. The
Inconnu have survived the Jyhad over many millennia. They can
take care of themselves, and, for that matter, you.

IV. Other Dwellers In Darkness

1. Lupines

These creatures inhabit the forests and other rural areas,
such as arboretums, swamps and college fraternity houses.
They rarely venture into the cities. Lupines are rarely dangerous unless they are provoked, so avoid provoking them.
Find out what areas the Lupines have claimed for themselves
and then avoid them at all costs; do no trespass in their
territory. If you become aware that any Kindred of your city
have trespassed in their territory, find a deep hole and
hide. If you have any contacts among the Gangrel, use them to
curry favors with the werewolves.Tell the Lupines that in
exchange for their help in rooting out your evil elders,
you'll work to create a pollution-free, perfect little world
where everyone lives in peace and harmony. They usually fall
for that.

Of course, you don't ever have to follow through on your
promises once you've reached princedom. After you are fin-
ished with the Lupines, ignore them. Who are they going to
complain to? Their elders? Yours? Keep ghouls packing silver
bullets on payroll and you'll be fine.

2. Mages

Assume that dealing with a mage will be like dealing with
a Tremere, only worse. These masters of the arcane arts are
as dangerous as any Kindred even though they are mortal. They
have their own concerns, though, and are generally too busy
chasing each other to bother us. Ignore the magi, and they
will most likely ignore you. If you cannot ignore a mage, and
your back is to the wall, strike hard, strike fast and strike
to kill. If they see you coming you're in a great deal of
trouble, but if you can strike the first blow it's usually
the last.

In your attempts to outflank your elders, you may make use
of those mages called Virtual Adepts. They are absolute wizards at the new methods of communicating, so far from the
pale of the elders. However, eventually they will turn on you
out of sheer boredom, so keep hard copies of your records off
line where they cannot get at them.

3. Wraiths

The Restless Dead, as they prosaically call themselves,
make superb spies. Invisible most of the time, intangible
always, they can hide within the home of the most paranoid
prince, all the while playing the fly on the wall. The trick,
of course, is making contact with them. Once you do start
talking with ghosts, however, it's often easy to strike a
deal. They all have concerns on earth which they're pathetically eager to have you protect. Don't cross them, however:
They may not seem potent but some can open coffins at midday
or rip souls from sleeping bodies.

A final warning: So far as I can tell, the Giovanni control them, so bear in mind that if you do traffic with these
restless spirits, everything you say will get back to the
Necromancers eventually.

4. Hunters

I recommend quietly getting out of their way. Hasty evacu-
ations leave signs, and keep the hunters on the trail.

If you can do so carefully, send them after your enemies.
This is trickier than it looks, and can be used as evidence
against you if it ever comes to light. So tread carefully,
and never let anyone else know that you use hunters as tools.
The unwritten rule, of course, is that if you use hunters on
others, you've just declared yourself fair game for hunters
to be used on you.

If you cannot avoid a hunter, then I offer to you as advice a tactic used by members of the Sabbat: Embrace the hunter in question, Blood Bond him and then send him off to go and kill the people who sent him. The irony alone makes it worth it.

A Last Note

A final word on any alliances you chose to make with your own kind: Be fair. Be up front. Never cheat. If you do cheat, your enemies will turn on you with a vengeance, and none will wish to be your friend. Keep your promises when it is polite and dispose of those who hold promises you cannot keep.

Watch out for the enemies secretly controlling your allies. Use your powers of Presence, but remember that loyalty gained from your own charisma and leadership is both hard to find and everlasting. However, also remember that no matter how charming you may be, Dominate beats a pair of aces.

V. Making your move

It will not be easy. On the other hand, it will not be agonizingly difficult. The day that you have waited for will simply arrive.

The day that you will make your move.

Everything that you have planned for, everything that you have prepared and every alliance forged leads to that crystallizing moment, the moment that you decide to take the princedom for yourself. Just how you intend to do it will be up to you. There is no surefire way to assume the title of prince. All that can be offered to you is advice, not on what to do, but on how you should do it.

The first thing to remember when making you move is that you must take your position in Kindred society. Power that is given by others can be taken away by others; power that you attain and take for yourself can only be lost by you. The only way you will impress the necessary elders (those elders you cannot control or kill are the elders you must impress — make sure that the number of elders you must impress is very small) is to take power. No appointments. No votes. No revolutionary councils. *Take* power.

We may delude ourselves (and I will admit that the elders of my own clan are the most guilty of this) into thinking that we can rule over ourselves by using traditions of government borrowed from the democratic traditions of the kine. But we are no longer mortal. We cannot rule ourselves according to mortals' rules and standards. The governmental traditions of the kine apply only to the mindset of the kine.

We are Kindred. We are ruled by the Beast. The hunger motivates us more than any other thing, no matter what lies we tell each other to delude ourselves. Our existences are taken up by the constant need to feed. This has affected our world view irrevocably. Remember, every Kindred looks out into the night and sees only the scarcity. Since we Kindred see world as a place of scarcity, one can only rule in this world by controlling the scarce resources. Remember this. If you make your move for power, everything that you do, as well as everything that your allies and enemies do, will be motivated by the need to protect and procure resources. You must make it very clear to all involved that you will maintain strict control of the resources that the Kindred are dependent on, and that loyalty to you will be most generously rewarded. You might wish to read *Beowulf* for pointers on this matter; notice how many useful swords Hrothgar gathers by dispensing useless gold rings.

The next point to remember is this: You must be sure of nothing less than total and absolute loyalty within your ranks. There can be no dissent, nor tolerance for those who have not committed themselves to your vision and cause. I am not saying that you must have fanatical followers, though that is a desirable option (look at how successful it has been for the Assamites), but you must have followers with no doubts about your cause. You must cast a very careful glance at all of your subordinates and allies, and it is best to eliminate any who so much as express doubt at crucial moments. Watch them, for if you see suspicious motivations or action among any of them, you will have to strike out for your own best interests. If you cannot trust a member of your own camp, you shall have to slay him. Quickly and ruthlessly is best, to serve as an example to your other followers. More importantly, this sends a message to your enemies as to how very serious you are.

Allies are best used during the *coup d'état*, but not trusted. Give them their instructions but do not rely upon them. You may end up simply using them as cannon fodder, or as a shield for your own troops. This sounds callous, but makes perfect sense. Churchill, after all, was willing to fight to the last Colonial during World War II; deceased Australian soldiers couldn't vote him out of office, but living British ones could keep him in.

Make your decision as to your relationship with each ally and then stick with it. Do not constantly change their standing with you. If an ally is treated as a trusted advisor one minute and a footsoldier the next, he will justifiably begin to suspect your motives as they regard him. Once that occurs, you may as well lead him to the prince's haven and turn him over. At best he'll no longer be of any help, and he may well betray you.

Many Kindred who have never taken power have romantic images of how they will achieve their coups. Some picture a genteel war of attrition, where the losing prince gracefully leaves the city. Others see a series of artfully handled political battle, climaxing with the exile of the prince on the word of the primogen and your being lead in triumph through the city streets.

It never happens this way.

A revolution is not neat. It is not tidy. It is a total and complete assault on all that has been established in an effort to create a more perfect order — yours — from the ashes. You are not fighting according to any known mortal rules of warfare, and the Jyhad has never bothered to stop and write down a set of guidelines. You are fighting a total and complete war for domination. You are fighting, like the wolf, for dominance, to become the alpha of the pack. However, we are more deceitful, more barbaric, crueler and nastier than any wolf could ever hope to be. We are Kindred. If you do not immediately throw all your resources at the prince you have decided to take down, have no doubt that he will feast upon your vitae. You must be smart, fierce and totally committed. You must also show no mercy. Absolutely none. Not ever. The moment you do, you are admitting weakness; the moment you admit weakness, you have already lost.

On what may be a more useful level, I suggest the following tactics once the situation develops into fighting in the streets:

Stir up troubles among the mortals as cover for what you are doing. The prince's forces will be split between keeping order, protecting the Masquerade and defending him against you. Your forces, on the other hand, will be focused on but one goal. After all, it's the prince's job to maintain the Masquerade, come what may.

Cut his lines of communication. Take down the advisors he trusts first, and he will be at a loss for advice and information. Once he starts striking at you blindly, he's yours.

Don't stop until he's dead. You should put out of your head all melodramatic notions of trials and sunrises. Kill him quickly and scatter his ashes. Don't diablerize him if there's the slightest possibility of witnesses, but if you can pull it off, I recommend it highly.

Once in power (and I assure you, it will seem as if it were but a moment to make your move, yet a lifetime to rule as an undisputed leader) you will need to plant the seeds for a firm and stable rule. I cannot give much advice here, as I only wish to tell you how to take power, not keep it. In truth, if you are truly worthy to rule, you shall know instinctively what must be done to assure a strong and steady rule. And if you are not worthy, you can be assured that your successor shall be arriving shortly.

Always remember that you must be willing to embrace the ideals of revolution, and then be just as willing to throw those ideals aside for the greater good of your realm. Once you have done this, you shall truly be a prince within your domain. Should you ever forget, well, the sunsets will be brighter for your ashes.

— A Friend

Rules and Regulations

REPORT FROM THE

St. Louis Conclave

CALLED INTO SESSION BY

Prince Jechid Del Monte

OF

Clan Ventrue

ON SEPTEMBER 17, 1995

My Most Honored Fellow Princes:

This letter is an abridged record of the conclusions, statements and other relevant information discussed at the St. Louis Conclave. It will be disseminated by courier to all princes of recognized Camarilla domains who were unable to attend, and to all non-aligned "princes" demonstrating either vulnerability or interest in an alliance. Most of the information contained within is merely a reaffirmation of what we have known for many years, but it is good to have it in codified form, I think.

Any questions, concerns or disagreements you may have can be directed back to the Ventrue Justicarate, care of the Archon Gabriel DiSantis, who is responsible for the Justicar's correspondence these days.

On the Position of the Prince Within his Domain

Traditionally, we Kindred have recognized the necessity of the prince to be the single most powerful Kindred within a given domain. This is the direct result of the need for order to be imposed by main strength on many occasions. When the whole of Kindred society was endangered by both the sheer number of Kindred competing for feeding grounds and by the lack of any established authority in a given area, it became a necessity to have a single potentate in place to provide direction for the safety of all.

During the Dark Ages, travel from city to city was perilous for mortals, let alone Kindred. The byways between various domains contained many dangers (especially from Lupines) and few shelters. In addition, the lord of a given domain was not required to give shelter or even safe passing to those entering, as for some reason many elders balked at what they considered to be a violation of their right to rule without competition from others of our kind. Eventually this sort of survival pressure led to the founding of our beloved Camarilla, and the initial codification of the rights of a ruler of any given domain.

Regrettably, many elders boycotted the fledgling organization, with some going so far as to become active enemies of the Camarilla. Those Kindred who persevered, however, came from the ranks of more enlightened elders and the ambitious ancillae of that time. Many of these farsighted souls are the leaders of the Camarilla this present night.

As the older, more conservative Kindred balked at the formation of a society of our kind, two events were happening that would solidify and strengthen the Camarilla: the increase in the size and numbers of the cities, and the growing ferocity of the Anarch Revolt.

As cities increased in size, Kindred came to these areas to feed off the quickly growing herds. The scope of Kindred society in those cities of the Middle Ages varied. Some cities were ruled much like other domains, by a single lord and his brood. Other metropolises would hold many members of various clans, resulting in intricate political maneuvering among the Damned in the never-ending quest for political supremacy. Often, one clan would be dominant in a given city —usually the Ventrue, Toreador or the Brujah — and interclan conflict led to many of the small brush fire wars of the period. Whenever a clan even briefly gained the upper hand in the maneuverings within a particular city, they would immediately seek to establish control over the city's ruling elite with the eventual goal of creating an unbreakable strangle hold on the city for their clan. Since those Kindred who were attempting such tactics were generally little more than ancillae at the time, many autonomous elders struck back by using their long-established control over the traditional ruling classes to wage war — economic and political — on the human and Kindred populace of the newly growing domains.

Materials for Study

For a prime example of this sort of stroke and counterstroke, see the treatise written by the Parisian Toreador Mercedes Guizot on the underlying stresses leading to the conflict between Henry of Navarre and the Catholic League. This conflict, occurring late in the Camarilla's consolidation period, is nonetheless representative of many similar, yet earlier conflicts. The League, supported by a small collective of pseudo-independent elders, through their influence on Henry III of Valois, was the epitome of the traditional elder-sponsored army. On the other hand, Navarre, through no fault of his own, had become a favorite of Guizot and as such became a particular target of the League's offensives. While the League won some initial victories, Guizot's request for Camarilla aid enabled Navarre, with his much smaller forces, to win decisive victories at Coutras, Arques and Paris. These triumphs, in addition to securing for Navarre the throne of France, also signaled the depositions of several of the elders behind the League. Guizot's treatise can be readily obtained by those interested, and it is highly recommended by this transcriber.

Those Kindred within many such threatened domains quickly joined with the Camarilla in an attempt to gain some measure of protection. Soon enough, the Camarilla was composed of many cities, leagues, councils and others who preferred sharing information and occasional action with their peers to the possibilities of death at the hands of the anarchs or submission to recalcitrant elders.

By the end of 16th century, the Camarilla was easily the largest sect of our kind extant. The benefits — information on the activities of the anarchs and the ability to travel safely from domain to domain — made it clear to many that membership in the Camarilla was the only reasonable guarantor of safety. It stands as a testament to the Camarilla's strength that, before the Sabbat Wars reached their height, the majority of those elders receiving Final Death during the Anarch Revolt were those who chose to stand against the Camarilla independently. The depredations of the anarchs took a heavy toll on those who spurned the safety of the Camarilla, and this lesson was not lost on those who survived. Most flocked to the Camarilla; a rare few instead swore allegiance to the newly-fledged Sabbat.

With the recognition of domains as political entities came the recognition of the position of prince. Initially, princedom was not a formal, official title granted by the Camarilla. Indeed, many domains held to their own political structures even after joining the Camarilla. Still, with the ever-increasing need to coordinate and gather information for passing along to other domains, it became necessary for at least one Kindred in each city to serve primarily as the Camarilla's eyes and ears. The title "Prince," in use for centuries among certain more self-aggrandizing vampiric rulers, rapidly spread across Europe as a name for the Kindred administrator for each city.

NOTE

The possibility was raised in discussion that the term was originally used in mockery of the primarily administrative function that the initial Camarilla princes performed. The term "Prince of the Vampires" could thus be seen as equivalent to the similarly satirical epithet "King of the Jews" bestowed upon Jesus Christ. However, as the only evidence extant for this theory comes from the personal memories of Brigd ni Dhomniall, the notoriously bad-tempered Brujah Prince of Cork, it was shelved for later discussion. Your transcriber only includes it here in the interest of completeness.

This individual would be responsible for looking out for the collective interests of the city's Kindred, as well as maintaining and enforcing the newly-minted Traditions. This Kindred also acquired responsibility for a sort of vampiric census, ascertaining how many Kindred were in any given region and their lineage. Eventually this role expanded to serving as the check-in point for visiting Kindred, which of course ensured that only the prince knew who was in the city at any given time. Knowledge is power, of course, and as knowledge became concentrated in the hands of these new princes, their power grew as well. Before long, there was no question as to which individual other Camarilla members would go to when entering a domain, or of whom Justicars made their demands. The prince, initially a mix of holdover tradition and derision, had become the true power in the Camarilla cities.

THE PRINCE AS DOMINANT POLITICAL FACTOR

As a matter of course, a prince must immediately establish both the authority with which she will maintain her rule, as well as the tone her rule will take. Will the prince be an autocrat, ruling with force and crushing opposition? Will she be a manipulator, setting her enemies at each other? Will she be a patriot, rallying her subjects against external threats? The style is almost irrelevant. What matters is that it be established at once, or else all is lost. Vacillation at the beginning of a prince's realm quickly turns into vacillation at the end of a very short reign. More importantly, setting the tone for a reign immediately means setting up the ground rules that everyone else in the city must play by or risk coming in conflict with the prince. Failure to do so means that she must play by the rules set up by her adversaries, and thus inevitably fall.

Recommendations of the Conclave on the Role of the Prince in the Modern Era

The main purpose of the Conclave, in addition to the exchange of information and posting of updates concerning the activities of Kindred considered a clear and present danger to the interests of the Camarilla, was to discuss and lay down new guidelines concerning the role of the prince in the modern era. Traditionally an office based on equal parts respect and fear, the princedom depends upon the prince's understanding of both her role in Kindred society and the tools at her disposal. The prince must also understand the unique dangers that our modern world offers. As an emissary of the Tremere of Washington D.C. domain put it: "The fires of the Inquisition are nothing compared to an atomic bomb; and Russia, until recently a center for Brujah power, has grown silent. The second largest stockpile of nuclear weapons on Earth is in the hands of unknowns. How many of us claim Havens in cities that are primary targets for such devices?" There is far more to worry about these days than Lupine incursions and the occasional curious mage.

In an effort to ease the burdens of ruling and encourage stability among the ruling class of the Kindred, the Conclave assembled information regarding the enemies, both supernatural and mundane that a prince might face. The Conclave also offered several recommendations on how a prince may more efficiently rule a domain, utilizing the powers and permissions implied in the Traditions. These recommendations were made to help new princes who had little experience, as well as to help more established princes reconcile their experience with the rapidly changing times.

RIGHTS AND PRIVILEGES

The prince has at his disposal many tools to insure a safe and prosperous reign. The rights of a prince are undisputed mastery over domain and the support of the Camarilla in the form of recognition of the right to rule that domain. The responsibilities of the prince are to maintain the Traditions, especially the Masquerade, as well as to inform the Justicars of the Camarilla of any and all threats, supernatural or otherwise.

The prince is faced with an enigma of ruling. She is given incredible power by her fellow Kindred with the implicit restriction that she will use the power given her to benefit her fellow Kindred. Fortunately, each prince has a specific set of guidelines for the maintenance of her domain, the six Traditions that were first given by Caine to his childer. If a prince is truly wise, she will recognize that the Traditions are the most powerful weapons at her disposal. The judicious use of that which is already at her disposal will enable the prince to ensure stability and the safety that the Camarilla requires to prosper. In the end, little else matters.

The Traditions

Each prince sets the agenda for his rule by how he chooses to interpret the Traditions. It falls to the prince to use the Traditions as his most potent resource. Appropriately wielded they can serve as just cause for quieting dissent and maintaining order. Improperly invoked, they can spark rebellion. The only power that a prince does not make for himself comes from maintaining the Traditions.

The First Tradition — The Masquerade

THOU SHALT NOT REVEAL THY TRUE NATURE TO THOSE NOT OF THE BLOOD. DOING SO SHALL RENOUNCE THY CLAIMS OF BLOOD.

For centuries, princes have used the enforcement of this Tradition to crush many of their enemies. What exactly constitutes a violation of the Masquerade is relative. Certain stricter princes argue that the creation of a ghoul can be interpreted as a violation, while others will look the other way at blatant transgressions under some circumstances. Many princes have been able to invoke the Masquerade in order to keep their own personal affairs private. A prince often has some leeway to interpret the Masquerade as suits his whim, and can frequently utilize breaks in the Masquerade — perceived or real — to intervene in just about any situation.

A prince is given the right to interpret the Masquerade as he sees fit. He should be aware however, that respect and fear for his authority will last only as long as he chooses to apply his interpretation of this Tradition evenly. If the prince is perceived as capricious or biased in his enforcement, those over whom the prince rules will question his authority. With questioning, of course, comes the beginning of defiance, and so on.

Recommendations of the Conclave: The Masquerade should, in these most careless times, be open to even stricter interpretation than before. In the past, the Masquerade was invoked to protect Kindred from the fires of the Inquisition. In this more modern era, the general potency of the Blood has weakened, while the weapons and tools available to the kine have become much more powerful. The Masquerade is in danger on a worldwide level, as the technological tools of the kine threaten to pierce the veil of shadows which we have thrown over ourselves.

In addition, it has become common practice for the Kindred to involve others that exist within the shadows — Lupines, mages, et al. — in the manipulations of the Jyhad. However, in these most dangerous of times, Kindred seeking to manipulate such beings are in fact making themselves vulnerable to those very creatures by revealing their existence. Dealings with other "supernatural" beings should henceforth be regarded as potential breaches of the Masquerade, should the prince wish to enforce them as such.

Princes are advised to maintain strict interpretations of the Masquerade, going as far as to invoke the final deaths of the violators if necessary. Those Kindred who openly associate with other supernatural beings without being closely monitored or sanctioned by the prince should be made an example of. The prince must invoke his authority in this matter, and report any potential tears in the fabric of the Masquerade to the Justicars.

The Second Tradition — The Domain

THY DOMAIN IS THY OWN CONCERN —
ALL OTHERS OWE THEE RESPECT WHILE IN IT.
NONE MAY CHALLENGE THY WORD
WHILE IN THY DOMAIN.

This Tradition guarantees to any Kindred that his claim on an area is recognized if that Kindred has the strength to hold it. The clans of the Camarilla have guaranteed this right to individual princes in exchange for the security that the prince provides. Under this system, individual clans need not waste their resources holding their protectorates against all others in an area, as the prince maintains the individual status of the clans. The prince performs this role by providing arbitration of disputes and recognizing and promoting the system of status, boons and Prestation.

The current interpretation of domain is that the prince has the leeway to set the boundary of the area he rules over. The prince may lay claim to a domain of any size, so long as he possess the power to exert his authority over the area in question. Claims of excessive domains may be challenged, of course.

A prince cannot rule a domain on his own. Traditionally, the prince relies upon those Kindred affiliated with and loyal to him (usually his brood) to control the various aspects of his domain, as well as calling upon the various elders to maintain their own control fiefdoms within the realm. The Brujah are often allowed to dominate the streets, the Toreador so-called high society, and the Gangrel those park lands not claimed by Lupines, and until recently this division of spheres of influence has served princes quite well.

However, now this semi-feudal system has led to a small crisis. Many Kindred, especially those new to the Blood, are convinced that since a prince has absolute control over a domain, he inevitably demonstrates favoritism in doling out Elysium status and feeding grounds to his most favored retainers. The youth of our community do not recognize that the prince is given his autonomy to do this by their own clans. For example, often the Nosferatu will recognize and support a prince in exchange for the implied autonomy that they will have in their underground realms. The same sort of barter system holds true for the other clans, as each clan and clan member will have established mini-domains within the realm that they wish the prince to leave alone.

The definition of domain, especially in this modern era, can be confusing. Some elders consider every aspect of a business to be a domain, though lax interpretations of the Tradition simply consider individual Havens to be domains out of common courtesy. The Tremere are the most avid supporters and interpreters of the Tradition of Domain, and one of the oldest established precedents in the Camarilla is that a Tremere Chantry is an individual domain accountable only to the clan. A prince who attempts to interfere in, or worse yet, force an issue within the Chantry invites the wrath of Vienna. This course of action is not recommended.

Recommendations of the Conclave: The prince is advised to give as well as take when it comes to domain. Recognizing that the elders of a realm each have an individual domain within his domain where they may freely pursue their individual goals in relative autonomy will win the respect of those elders. Subsequently, the prince will find that, rather than giving away his city, he has strengthened his rule. Those elders controlling an area, so long as they respect the prince's authority, will police themselves (and each other) much more fiercely and efficiently than the prince ever could. The prince will also ensure loyalty by maintaining the illusion of having "given" an area of a domain to a particular elder, making an elder thankful and loyal for what was already his and charging that elder with administrating it in the prince's name. Not every elder will accept such a rule, instead waiting to make their move. In this case a prince should never hesitate to eliminate such elders. This maintains the impression that the elder's power is the prince's to give and receive.

The Third Tradition — The Progeny

**THOU SHALT SIRE
ONLY WITH THE PERMISSION OF THINE ELDER.
IF THOU CREATEST ANOTHER WITHOUT THINE ELDER'S LEAVE,
BOTH THOU AND THY PROGENY SHALL BE SLAIN.**

This is the most ironclad of the Traditions. The power of the prince is dependent on how tightly he holds to this Tradition. If a prince is too restrictive, he will frustrate the Kindred within his domain. This results in progeny being created without his permission, or outside his domain, and then turned loose as a challenge to his authority. If a prince is too lenient, the number of progeny in a domain will explode and produce inevitable conflicts. Fights over feeding grounds, herds and position will result from such a population increase, threatening the stability of the prince's reign.

Recommendations of the Conclave: The prince must establish a firm policy on progeny, as any deviation from an initially declared policy will bring allegations of favoritism and spark revolt. Conclusively and quickly answering the many questions raised — Are ghouls considered progeny? — is a must, else those concerns will fester. There are other matters that must be taken into account as well. Specifically, a prince must be careful not to create a large brood while restricting the rights of others to Embrace, as nothing will alienate the primogen faster than being out-bred, as it were, by the one whose power they are supposedly balancing.

The Fourth Tradition — The Accounting

**THOSE THOU CREATEST ARE THINE OWN CHILDREN,
UNTIL THY PROGENY SHALL BE RELEASED,
THOU SHALT COMMAND THEM IN ALL THINGS.
THEIR SINS ARE THINE TO ENDURE.**

The interpretation of this Tradition has varied across the centuries. The most frequently invoked interpretation is also one of the strictest: Any Kindred must be responsible for the actions of his or her direct progeny until such time as that progeny's release into Kindred society. There have been different applications of the Fourth Tradition, however. Some princes, particularly on the Continent, have made it a point to hold clan leaders responsible for the actions of any and all clan members within their domain, regardless of lineage. Only the most powerful and secure princes have been able to invoke this interpretation of the Fourth Tradition, but when clan elders have to answer for the actions of their more rambunctious constituents, it is amazing just how infrequently a prince has to sully his hands with day-to-day discipline problems. The theory behind such accountability is simple: If an individual Kindred claims leadership of his clan, coterie, etc., that Kindred must also face the punishments for transgressions of individual members or else relinquish leadership. Those princes who have implemented this type of interpretational ethic have reported some success after initial resistance, as clan leaders are more concerned with maintaining their own safe and secure status quo than in getting hauled up before the prince every time a neonate makes a misstep.

Recommendations of the Conclave: Responsibility and accountability must be the hallmarks of Kindred society. Many Kindred will balk at an overly strict interpretation of the Fourth Tradition, and many princes attempting to implement such interpretations will be in for more trouble than they bargained for. However, as the millennium approaches, princes are advised to impress upon those Kindred within their domains the importance of taking responsibility, both for their own actions and the actions of those they choose to represent. This caveat must also apply to princes. The age when a prince could rule over his domain in complete ignorance of most of his subjects is fading rapidly. Ignorance is no excuse for not addressing the problems of a domain, and looking the other way cannot be tolerated in these dangerous times.

The Fifth Tradition — Hospitality

**HONOR ONE ANOTHER'S DOMAIN.
WHEN THOU COMEST TO A FOREIGN CITY,
THOU SHALT PRESENT THYSELF TO THE ONE WHO RULETH THERE.
WITHOUT THE WORD OF ACCEPTANCE, THOU ART NOTHING.**

This Tradition is the cornerstone of the Camarilla, and its interpretation is as strict now as ever. There are an increasing number of Kindred who flaunt their mobility, leading to tremendous difficulties in ascertaining which Kindred are where, when. With so many advances in transportation, it is difficult to keep track of the movements of many ancillae and neonates. Journeys that used to take months through Lupine-infested woods now take mere hours on Harley-Davidsons. In the face of a quickly shrinking world, this Tradition must remain sacrosanct. Without knowledge, a prince has no power. Without knowledge of who resides in his domain, a prince cannot control that domain. Hence, the Fifth Tradition must be upheld with more vigor, lest the sanctity of a prince's domain, the very foundation of the Camarilla, crumble before the technological onslaught.

Recommendations of the Conclave: There will always be minor offenders against this Tradition, but in these threatening times such laxity cannot be tolerated. Any Kindred caught in violation of this Tradition who can be made an example of, *must* be made an example of. A prince who is not sought out for introduction is a prince ignored. A prince ignored will not be feared. A prince who is not feared is a prince deposed.

On a practical level, princes should enlist their subjects' assistance in enforcing this Tradition. Demonstrating appreciation for subjects who help newcomers to present themselves is recommended, as sufficient eventual remuneration will keep Kindred eyes open for newcomers, including those who may not want their presence known.

The Sixth Tradition — Destruction

THOU ART FORBIDDEN TO DESTROY ANOTHER OF THY KIND. THE RIGHT OF DESTRUCTION BELONGETH ONLY TO THINE ELDER. ONLY THE ELDEST AMONG THEE SHALL CALL THE BLOOD HUNT.

A prince may only rule so long as a prince is feared. A prince is feared only so long as he is willing to crush all — friend or foe — who violate the Traditions. The Blood Hunt is often a means of last resort, and those Kindred who have the Blood Hunt called upon them are often such a great threat that they must be made an example of. Others, sad to say, are the victims of political fortune. The one factor that unites all Blood Hunts is that they are a device of political expediency. If a prince wants to make an example out of a particular Kindred, calling a Blood Hunt to show his power is the best way to do so. Simultaneously, the prince crushes the offender and demonstrates the folly of disobeying the prince's authority.

Recommendations of the Conclave: A Blood Hunt must *never* be called lightly, nor should a prince believe that her entire domain will rise in arms against the perpetrator. A prince must be ever-vigilant to the possible consequences of the calling of a Blood Hunt. While many younger licks may readily partake in such activity for the excitement and opportunity it offers, there is a possibility that a great deal of jockeying for position, power and influence will take place behind the scenes, producing casualties besides the intended one.

This is especially likely if the target of the hunt had any assets that were valuable. A prince may find that the elders within her domain are too busy feeding upon the carcass of her enemy to notice or care about the specific reasons for the calling of the Blood Hunt — and that is the inherent danger in calling the Hunt. When the Blood Hunt becomes a means by which ambitious Kindred may advance their agenda rather than a sentence of doom for disobedience, a prince will find herself ruling a bloodthirsty mob that demands that she invoke this power for the slightest transgression. In this situation, the prince is no longer feared. Indeed, as the elders are happily devouring each other, the prince who accommodates their every whim becomes an object of scorn and ridicule. To maintain its proper effect, a Blood Hunt must be invoked rarely, yet with power. The Lextalionis must be held as sacred by all Kindred, and it falls on the shoulders of the prince to make this so. Familiarity in all things, even the Blood Hunt, breeds contempt.

When invoking Blood Hunt, it is recommended that a prince have hard evidence readily available in case the rationale for the Hunt is questioned. It may be necessary to manufacture this evidence, but that is the work of an hour, and witnesses can be Dominated or otherwise made convincing. It is best for the prince if problem Kindred can be removed without invoking the Blood Hunt. However, it is recommended that this action be performed by the prince herself in the utmost secrecy (save when an example is being made), so that an enemy finds a minimum of skeletons in the closet.

Advisories on Enemies of the Camarilla

A second reason for the convocation of the Conclave was to create an opportunity for Camarilla members to advise and inform one another about potential allies and enemies. The changes in mortal society within the last century alone have produced a great many new threats. When these new enemies are added to the new tactics and technologies to which the old enemies of the Camarilla now have access, the inevitable conclusion that is reached is that this is a time of unprecedented danger. The Conclave feels the urgent need to address these threats and offer recommendations for all members to follow *vis-à-vis* dealing with them in the most efficient manner possible.

THE SABBAT

This sect remains the most dangerous foe of the Camarilla, and few princes have not had some sort of encounter with the Sabbat. We have been collecting data on these Kindred since their initial formation, and many Conclaves and councils of war have been held on this one subject alone.

Recommendations of the Conclave: Any incursion by Sabbat vampires must be halted before it begins. Sabbat presence in a city tends to increase exponentially, thus the sooner it is detected, the easier it is to eradicate. On the other hand, McCarthyistic tactics are most definitely not recommended, as heavy-handed tactics tend to drive disaffected anarchs directly into the Sabbat's arms. It is vital that tight control of a city's media be maintained during a Sabbat attack; passing off their crimes and breaches of the Masquerade as the actions of a "serial killer" works well.

It is recognized that individual Sabbat vampires may successfully infiltrate a domain for years, subverting and destroying from within while passing information to their sect's leaders. Princes are advised to do all in their power to find and destroy these spies, as they pose a far greater threat than dozens of their so-called "Crusades." A dozen poorly-planned assaults can be beaten off easily, but one well-planned one, abetted by a traitor, stands a much higher chance of succeeding.

ANARCHS

If the Sabbat are the dagger pointed at our throats, the anarchs are the bomb waiting to explode underneath us. The anarchs as a whole have no unified voice or power base, relying on their numbers and unpredictability to eke out whatever victories they may. Even their stronghold, Los Angeles, remains a city divided by petty disputes. The anarchs have ferocity and a certain brute strength, but are too lost in their own rhetoric generally to be much of a threat. In truth, most sensible Kindred consider the anarchs to be lapsed Camarilla just going through a rebellious phase. Still, they are capable of deadly tantrums.

Recommendations of the Conclave: Anarchs make excellent cannon fodder, particularly if you can convince them that your war is theirs. Set up a shadow enemy for them to fight and they'll too busy to attack you directly. Then, when real danger threatens, remove the shadow. They'll thank you and gladly die for you, without ever knowing that they've been had. Elder anarchs have shown time and time again that they will sell out their own brethren in exchange for secure feeding grounds or such like privileges. Much of their rancor against their elders is poorly-disguised envy, and this can be exploited.

ASSAMITES

This clan of diabolists has made no secret of its contempt both for the Camarilla and our Traditions. However, they have held themselves accountable to the Treaty of Tyre, thanks to the efforts of our Tremere. Openly resentful of the Camarilla and its power, the Assamites yet show a healthy respect for the collective power the Camarilla can muster. Perhaps the memory of the infiltration of Alamut is yet fresh with them. Only the Tremere have much to worry about from the Assamites as a group. Otherwise, the danger from the Assassins lies on the individual level. Even members of our own sect are not above hiring the Assamites to perform assassinations, and many princes have fallen to their blades.

Recommendations of the Conclave: The Assamites are powerful allies and dangerous enemies. A prince must not interfere with an individual Assamite and his affairs, lest that prince find himself unwittingly making for himself a place in those affairs. A wise prince can make good use of Assamite talents, either employing them as bodyguards or by sending them against non-Camarilla rivals. Contracting fellow Camarilla members is, of course, expressly forbidden. A prince must make sparing use of the Assamites, however lest he find himself either indebted to the Assassins or too dependent on them for tasks which he ought to be capable of performing himself. Princes dependent upon Assamites tend to have reigns that are both brief and bloody, as the subjects of such a prince will take it upon themselves to remove him for the sake of the peace of the city.

FOLLOWERS OF SET

This clan has made no secret of its intention to establish worldwide dominion at the expense of their fellow Kindred. It is clear that of all the non-aligned clans of the Kindred, the Followers of Set pose the greatest threat to the security of the Camarilla. While individual princes have in the past tolerated the Followers of Set as a "lesser evil" when compared to the Sabbat, this has resulted in the unchecked spread of the Setites across the world. They have established power bases in nearly all of our cities even as unwary princes congratulate themselves on having supposedly used the Snakes as a buffer against the Sabbat.

The Followers of Set have proven themselves to be dangerous, subtle manipulators of both Camarilla and kine. They traffic in favors and addictions, and make a point of subverting as many Kindred as possible to their perverted wills. These enthralled Kindred then implement the Setite agenda. The effect in the end is the same as if the Sabbat has overrun the city: blood in the streets and another fallen prince.

Recommendations of the Conclave: The Followers of Set are to be destroyed when possible, but always quickly and quietly. At this point, the Setites are too powerful and too well entrenched in many be fought directly. Furthermore, a concealed campaign restricts the opportunities Setite pawns have to inform on or sabotage anti-Setite efforts. In addition, the Snakes can mobilize their human pawns to create severe threats to the well-being of any city, thus threatening the Masquerade and distracting resources from the campaign against the Setites.

Most Kindred within a domain see the Followers of Set as little more than the suppliers of guns and drugs, and this is where the danger lies. Utilizing the Setites as a primary supplier threatens to make the Camarilla dependent on the clan for many resources — resources that can be taken away at the worst possible time. Restrict access to Setite-controlled areas, take every opportunity to eliminate individual Setites without resorting to Blood Hunts or the like, and above all do not deal with them, even *in extremis*. The price is always too high. As Kipling put it, "Once one pays the Danegeld, one never gets rid of the Dane."

Giovanni

This clan has kept a respectable and quiet appearance over the centuries. The unfortunate Cappadocian incident has made it impossible fully to integrate them into the Camarilla, yet in many affairs, we have had good relations with the Necromancers. There has been friction on an individual level in the past between members of the Giovanni and individual princes, but such incidents have always been isolated. The Giovanni always attempt to work well with the prince of any city they occupy, in the cogent belief that strife is bad for business. They will hold to their ancient pledge to remain neutral, while many more entrepreneurial Kindred have had success in working with them. Still, it should not be forgotten that they do have their own agenda, and should a prince thwart it, they will attempt to remove him summarily.

Recommendations of the Conclave: A prince is advised to work with the Giovanni presence in the city to ensure that they won't be actively moving against him. It is both easier and safer to attempt to dissuade a Giovanni from a course of action than to attempt simply to stop him. It is best to have multiple contacts within the clan, so that if you are forced to deal with one permanently, you have a channel through which you can justify your "no doubt necessary" actions to Venice.

Ravnos

These gypsies have made their contempt for the Camarilla and its ways well-known. Fortunately, they are not an overt threat to the Camarilla, nor do they endanger the Masquerade. As such, the Ravnos only occupy a place on this list due to their open defiance of the Camarilla's authority. Very few Ravnos will bother to present themselves, and those who do have usually pocketed something valuable on their way out. In addition, it is difficult to tell if a particular individual encountered is a Ravnos or an *antitribu*, and the latter will play up this confusion for all it is worth.

Recommendations of the Conclave: A prince is advised to treat all individual Ravnos as if they were potentially in the employ of the Sabbat. It is a common Sabbat tactic to send Ravnos *antitribu* on scouting missions to Camarilla-held domains, and they don't seem to have realized that this tactic was uncovered and countered long ago. Non-Sabbat Ravnos should be handled with kid gloves and gently ushered from the city, lest they invite some of their fellow clan members to join their fun. Calling Blood Hunt on Ravnos is inevitably more trouble than it is worth, and it can produce a devastating retribution.

LUPINES

The Lupine presence *around* most domains is inescapable, and poses a problem for most princes. While it is rare for Lupines to take a city by storm, they can certainly restrict access for our kind to any place they choose. Any attempt to mount a sally against the encircling Lupines usually ends in disaster due to the superior strength of each individual werewolf. Additionally, the Lupines are capable of gathering their numbers with astonishing speed, and apparently have the impetus of religious fanaticism behind their desire to wipe us from the planet. All in all, they make a most dangerous foe.

For example, witness the recent train of events in Chicago. Lodin, then prince, foolishly called a Blood Hunt on every Lupine in the city. While there were gains at first, the savage ferocity and sheer numbers of the Lupine counterattack forced the primogen (after the destruction of the prince) to sue for peace. To this night, the situation remains tenuous in Chicago, yet it serves as a reminder for Kindred that the Lupines, even with their numbers dwindling, are still a very real threat.

Recommendations of the Conclave: The Lupine presence has traditionally been limited to the countryside. There are Lupines who choose to live in the city, but they remain a distinct minority. The best way to combat the Lupines should they pose a threat remains the same as always: Cut down their forests, pollute their rivers, set up some anarchs to take the blame for you, and conveniently leave town on business when they finally organize themselves enough to attack. The Lupines have short memories, and if they cannot find their enemies, they will attack whatever is in front of them instead. A prince can best defeat the Lupine by maintaining a strict Masquerade, observing their actions from a safe distance. The late Lodin's confrontational tactics have proven an unprecedented disaster, and should a prince wish to emulate them, we would request a list of his next of kin to notify as to his incipient demise.

A Final Note

This letter was compiled in the express hope of sharing the insights of the Kindred gathered at the St. Louis Conclave. It is the intention of this letter to provide the princes of the Camarilla and interested elders with updated, relevant information concerning the role of princedom in Camarilla society, and the stresses unique to princes in the modern era. This letter summarizes the results of the debates, presentations, symposiums and other activities of the Conclave, and is intended as a fair and open representative of the conclusions reached by the Conclave participants.

Princes of Note

Siegfried, Prince of Vancouver

This ancient Ventrue was originally a Visigoth chieftain. His sire, a Roman consul named Regulus, offered the chieftain the chance for immortality, but didn't tell him the terms. When the chieftain realized he had become one of the Draugar (the Undead), he slew his sire in a fit of rage and then drank the blood from his heart. The Ventrue pursued him across Europe for his crime, but never brought him to justice. For his part, Siegfried was quite content to exist outside of the clan. He never chose to accept the Ventrue or their traditions, instead deciding to forge his own path.

Remaining aloof from Kindred politics, Siegfried chose an existence as a wanderer. Eventually his travels led him to the west coast of North America. Here he found an untamed land that would be perfect for him to establish his domain and remain safe from the Jyhad. Using his powers of persuasion and the financial capital that he had accumulated over the centuries, he set about building and expanding the human settlements in the area. This was no easy task, as there were constant attacks from the Lupines and their Native American allies in an attempt to stem the tide of European migration. However, the Visigoth beat them all back and used his growing international influence to encourage the city's growth. He used his own finances to bankroll many of the city's first industries, walked its borders at night to protect it from incursion, and protected the kine living within the

*Note: Siegfried first appeared in **Dark Alliance: Vancouver**

Siegfried, Prince of Vancouver

city during the dark and cold first nights of the city's existence. His influence enabled Vancouver to grow into one of the largest cities in Canada. Many other princes are envious of just how much control and autonomy Seigfreid has been able to assert over his city, but they do not see the painstaking work that he put into its creation. Siegfried is not just the Prince of Vancouver, he is also its founder and protector.

In fact, Siegfried did not declare himself prince until the 1940s. He had been content to remain in the background, allowing Vancouver to become a neutral ground between the warring factions of Kindred. Unfortunately, this attracted the attention of the anarchs, who began to use the city as a staging base in their war for the cities of the west coast. Realizing that he was facing a very real war between the Camarilla and the anarchs in the middle of a city he had helped to create, he declared himself prince to forestall the conflict. He also instituted a set of harsh laws that broke the power of the clans within the city while providing comfort and security for those that chose to accept the prince's rule. This ensured him a docile, unified populace with which to face the resurgent Lupine threat.

The harshness of the prince's laws and the brutality with which they were enforced enabled Vancouver to become a rarity in Kindred society; Vancouver is ruled only by its prince. There is no open help from the primogen or other clan leaders, or from the other clans, for that matter. His rule is recognized neither by the Camarilla nor the Sabbat. Vancouver has attained the status of a neutral city where any Kindred may petition the prince to stay so long as they choose to accept his laws. It is also one of the few cities that has successfully maintained peace with the Lupines.

Siegfried has also cultivated his personal power. Several princes owe boons to him, and the peace that he has enforced in the city has impressed the elders of the Camarilla. Though they are loath to admit it, the Justicars of the Camarilla consider Siegfried's success in Vancouver a standard against which all other princes should model their efforts.

Dr. Alexander Meuser, Prince of Jerusalem

During the Zionist movement of the late 19th century, many European intellectuals were swept up in the excitement of the movement dedicated to creation of a Jewish homeland. One such intellectual was Dr. Meuser. A philosopher and speaker on such issues, he traveled across Europe rallying support for the Zionist movement.

His intelligence, combined with his ferocity and zeal at debating, attracted the attention of a Brujah elder. Meuser was Embraced, and once certain political realities were pointed out to him, he became just as fierce a warrior in the Jyhad as he had been for Jerusalem. Of particular interest to Meuser were the similarities between the Jewish people and the Brujah: Both had been crushed by Rome; both were deliberately misunderstood by the society around them; and both wanted to re-create or reclaim their home. Meuser soon became intrigued at the idea of combining the two goals, possibly reestablishing a society based upon Brujah ideals in the Holy Land.

Meuser's activities continued during the 20th century as he led bands of Zionists in fighting against the British occupation of Palestine and the Ventrue "administrators" who occupied the land. With the onset of World War II, he devoted himself to helping escapees from the camps make *aliyah*, or immigrate to Palestine.

After World War II, Meuser used the status and influence that he had gained to assert power over Jerusalem and what would later become known as Israel. The British Ventrue had attempted in their usual colonial fashion to rule over the Palestinians and had met with unprecedented failure. Both the politicking of various Inconnu and the Setites were to blame for this failure, but Meuser was more concerned with mortal affairs. Instrumental in the creation of the State of Israel, he asserted himself as prince and began working to develop the Israeli nation and provide for its people.

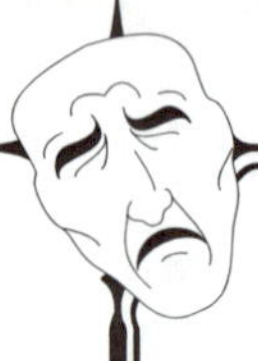

Dr. Alexander Meuser

To the other ancients, he portrayed himself not as a ruler, like the British Ventrue had, but as a diplomat of the Camarilla's interests in the region. This move proved to be politically successful, reassuring the Camarilla bluenoses that Meuser's power was titular only, and that Kindred affairs of the city were in the hands of the city's much older, more acceptable inhabitants. While Meuser had weakened himself politically, his figurehead status as prince left the responsibility of maintaining the Traditions to the city's elders. In the meantime, Meuser was free to build alliances, mediate disputes and otherwise build a real power base for himself.

During the Cold War, Meuser and his domain faced incredible violence as the region's factionalism and brush fire wars flared out of control. In addition to the many different clans of the Camarilla, Meuser found that his domain included a large population of Assamites and Setites. Occasional incisions of anarchs and Sabbat added to the volatility of the mix. These Kindred seemed only concerned with their own goals, and they increased the amount of violence in the area to an unimaginable extent. Many Kindred who were Embraced in the area also chose to bring their rivalries with them beyond the grave. It was — and still is — not unusual to see Israeli Brujah and Ventrue fighting fiercely against their Palestinian counterparts.

In the face of the strife, Meuser stuck to his agenda. He did not attempt to exert his power, instead relying on subtle alliances that he had forged with the Kindred ancients of Jerusalem. All of the following were subtly drawn to Meuser's banner: a coterie of Ventrue who were Embraced during the Crusades, a brood of Nosferatu Noddists who wished to excavate the catacombs deep beneath the city in search of clues about the second city, and a substantial population of Brujah idealists who saw in the city a possibility of rebuilding Carthage. Combining this potent coalition with his sway over the Israeli government, Meuser found his rule to be far smoother than he had any right to expect.

Meuser's rule has not been without adversity. His successes and failures have mirrored the modern history of Israel in the Gothic-Punk world. The current peace plan for the Middle East is reflective of Meuser's efforts, but the recent assassination of Yitzhak Rabin highlights his inability to completely control his domain. Violence between Jews and Arabs once again threatens. The Ventrue elders, a coterie of Knights Templar Embraced during the Crusades, wish to renew their off again-on again war with the Assamites. And Meuser is convinced that the Followers of Set exert far more control over the Israeli government than he had previously been led to believe. Still, he walks the halls of the *Knesset*, doing his best for both his peoples in even the darkest hours.

Robert Pedder, Prince of Hong Kong

The prince, or *Tai Pan*, as he is known within his own domain, has shaped the growth and expansion of the British Colony of Hong Kong throughout its history. He began his presence in the city by exerting control over the trading ventures. His mortal family, one of the more powerful British merchant houses, had traveled to Hong Kong with the British during the Colonial Era. For this reason he was Embraced, and whatever control he exerted over the city's trade as a mortal was only increased after his death. From his control over trade in the colony, Pedder increased and diversified his influence. Eventually he gained control over all aspects of the colony's government and transportation sectors, which in turn led to control of the city in its entirety.

The *Tai Pan* has a sizable brood which helps him to rule over his domain. He has worked hard to make his rule over the city both peaceful and profitable, and if he were ruling over any other city, his success and accomplishments would make him one of the most powerful princes in the Camarilla. Unfortunately, the vagaries of mortal politics affect his rule.

In 1997, the city of Hong Kong will revert control back to China, and to many of the Kindred in the city, this means that the mysterious Asian vampires are ready to take the city by force. In the past few years, Pedder has

***Note:** Pedder first appeared in **A World of Darkness.**

Robert Pedder

noted some disastrous encounters his own forces have had with mysterious vampires from the mainland. While he has offered to share his observations with the rest of the Camarilla, no one else has anything to add to what he already knows. His enemy, then, remains an unknown.

Reduced to watching as his very domain systematically flees the island, Pedder sees many of the elders of the city are moving their resources and herds else where. Many of the more recent Kindred arrivals are setting up quick ventures and then abandoning the city once they've made a pile of cash. As 1997 looms closer, Pedder is forced to watch as all he has built is systematically dismantled. He is also faced with the loss of status that comes from no longer being prince. Few princes in the Camarilla have ever given up a domain, yet this is exactly what Pedder is being forced to do.

The Ventrue are not ignorant of his plight, however. Pedder has long held a sterling reputation within the clan for his quiet, consistent service. His accomplishments in ruling and maintaining a domain in such a hostile area have given Pedder an enviable reputation among the elders of his clan. Pedder is already the front-runner to become the next Ventrue Justicar; many whisper that it is a consolation prize for the loss of his beloved city of Hong Kong.

His Eminence and Benevolent Grace, Lord Magnus Rex Mundi

Of all the princes of the Camarilla, none is as famous among his peers as His Royal Eminence, Lord Magnus. The reputation of Lord Magnus precedes him. Depending upon which tales you hear, he is a soon to be member of the Inconnu, he has battled the Sabbat, Black Hand, and the Lupines, he has fought mages, he is friends with all the Justicars, and the Inner Circle of the Camarilla regularly consult him for advice.

And if you listen to the people who know the truth, you will also learn that he does not exist.

Lord Magnus is believed to have been the brain child of a coterie of Malkavian and Toreador Harpies who sought to embarrass the current prince of their city. Lord Magnus, a so-called ancient Ventrue, soon "appeared" (via an ancilla's Obfuscate powers) walking around the Elysium, sending letters to the primogen declaring himself the new prince, and basically acting like a pompous, foolish parody of the target of the Harpies' ire.

The results of the prank were not unexpected. Humiliated, the prince attempted to destroy this " Lord Magnus" and anyone associated with him. The primogen remained silent, yet it soon became clear that they were subtly

supporting the coterie who had created the phantom. The prince became a laughingstock within his own city, and was soon removed from power. His work done, Lord Magnus disappeared.

However, word of the mysterious Lord Magnus soon spread, and letters from the mysterious elder soon appeared in other cities as well. Lord Magnus soon began to pop up all over the world, his every incarnation a pompous parody of the prince of whatever city he appeared in.

Lord Magnus regularly sends letters to the Justicars, giving his advice on the state of Kindred affairs. He appears at regular intervals in both New Orleans and Rio de Janeiro for Mardi Gras. The Prince of Rio de Janeiro has even appointed Lord Magnus as Seneschal and reserves a suite of hotel rooms for him when he arrives. Where and when Lord Magnus will show up is a mystery, but Magnus sightings are always a social event, much like the Kindred equivalent of watching for the Loch Ness monster.

At present, it is rumored that a secret group of Toreador, Malkavians, Brujah, Ravnos and even some Tremere and Ventrue are responsible for staging sightings of Lord Magnus. His appearances are always designed to criticize and ridicule a harsh, unpopular or unwise prince. Some princes have failed to get the joke, and Blood Hunts have been called on Lord Magnus in no fewer than nine cities. Most princes can gauge the relative popularity of their reign by whether or not Lord Magnus appears in their domain.

The phantom only remains for as long as he is paid attention to. He will sometimes stay in an area for months at a time, other times for only a few weeks. There is no pattern to his appearances that can be discerned, and this is part of his power.

Lord Magnus has acquired mythic status in Kindred society. In fact, Lord Magnus sightings are the Kindred equivalent of Elvis sightings, with one lick or another claiming to have met the mysterious elder in convenience stores or Elysiums. Lord Magnus appears infrequently, though his most recent appearance was at the St. Louis Conclave, where his letter (which detailed, among other things, how primogen should be ignored or actively persecuted by most princes. In addition, it postulated that a prince could ignore violations of the Traditions if his own lackeys were involved) was read to the members of the assembly and considered for inclusion in the report to be filed with the Justicars. The Conclave thanked Lord Magnus for his advice, and Lord Magnus announced that he would be spending the next few years studying with the Inconnu, all of whom are his close personal friends.

Christian, Brujah Elder

An outspoken enemy of the very concept of princedom and the author of *A Manifesto on Becoming Prince*, Christian was a fervent believer in the Anarch Revolt. Fanatical in his devotion, when the leaders of the revolt chose to submit to the whim of the Camarilla elders, Christian was crushed. He swore that he would never give up the fight and tromped off to carry on his one-vampire war. Furthermore, he swore to crush his contemporaries, especially former anarchs, by supporting revolt behind the scenes.

He nearly joined with the Sabbat, the rumor runs, but decided against taking the chance of having his associates sell him out again. Cut off from every sect, Christian soon became the self-appointed enemy of the status quo in Kindred society, appearing in any area where the prince was felt to be particularly unjust. His harsh manner has made him many enemies, and Christian wears the number of Blood Hunts called on him by various princes as a badge of pride. However, Christian has never been reprimanded by his own clan, since he has repeatedly maintained that he will willingly recognize any authority that is just. Of course, Christian has his own idea of what constitutes a just authority.

Christian has currently found himself the prince of a respectably sized city in the midwestern United States. His ascension to the princedom was not intentional, but came as the result of a sudden Sabbat assault, during which he was instrumental in fighting off the invasion. Ironically, as the newly appointed prince, Christian now finds himself in the same position he has criticized so harshly. He also knows that he is being watched by the elders of the Camarilla, and, due to his past, Christian knows he will be held to his own claims on how a prince should rule.

Experience the undead at the height of their power. **Vampire: The Dark Ages** takes you to the twelfth century, when the Kindred ride as lords. Unfettered by any Masquerade, they build kingdoms and bathe in blood. Glory and terror await in the shadows of the past...but beware, the darkness you need fear most is the darkness within yourself.

Vampire: The Dark Ages is a hardbound
stand-alone game that is completely compatible
with Vampire: The Masquerade.
Coming in Spring, 1996

BRUBAKER
95
LAWS OF THE NIGHT
The Pocket Guide to Mind's Eye Theatre.
All the Rules.
All the Clans.
All the Disciplines.
All Together.
JULY